CHRISTMAS EVE

by Lori Osterberg

Christmas Eve/ Lori Osterberg.

Chapter One

Eve Nichols scrunched up the piece of paper and threw it at the window in front of her. She placed her elbows on her desk, and dropped her head between her fingers, massaging her temples.

Normally the rain didn't get to her. She'd lived in Seattle most of her adult life. But lately, it was getting harder to take.

Up on the twenty-third floor, the view could be spectacular on a clear day. Today, it was nothing but clouds.

Two more weeks, she told herself. Two more weeks and her daughter would be home for Christmas. Then she'd have two glorious weeks with twenty-one-year-old Grace.

She glanced at the photo on the corner of her desk. It was the two of them together, taken a few months before, when they'd traveled to Bali. Eve had treated them to a two-week trip a few weeks before Grace had left for her junior year of college.

Grace was spending the year studying abroad in Granada, Spain.

Eve picked up the photo and thought about their time together. They hadn't done much, other than enjoy the pool and local cuisine. They'd read a dozen books. Eaten more than they should have. Enjoyed spa visits several times a week. They'd headed out on a few bike tours given by the hotel staff. But mostly they'd talked for hours, about life and what they each wanted in the future.

For Grace, it seemed easy. She had very clear goals. She wanted her degree in International Relations and Modern Languages. She wanted a job that would take her to the far corners of the world, to work as an international aid worker or foreign relations. Eve knew as determined as she was, she would get it. She was hoping her year abroad would help her secure an internship for the upcoming summer. Grace was already starting to apply.

Eve put the photo down and stared out at the clouds one more time.

How had time gone so fast? How had she fallen into a

life she was no longer happy with, yet had no idea how to change it?

Part of it could be blamed on her ex. They'd divorced six years before, when Grace was a freshman in high school. He'd come home one day and said he was meant for bigger things. He had only so much life left, and he no longer wanted to live it with her.

Translation: he wanted sex with younger women. Eve had figured that out right away. She drew the line two months after they'd separated when his twenty-four-year-old girlfriend came to pick up Grace instead of him. She filed for divorce that same day, and was officially single a few months later.

She hadn't dated until Grace had gone off to college. She needed that time to recover. But once it was just her and too much space in her empty nest, she'd started thinking about someone new. Someone who could make her feel human again.

"Hey, Larry just brought in a cake for December birthdays. We're meeting in the conference room in five. Come on, birthday girl. Since your birthday's coming up, we can't start without you."

Eve twirled her chair around to nod at Hannah, her personal assistant, standing in her doorway. She blinked a few times, trying to pull herself back into the present.

"What kind of cake did he get?" Cake was just what she needed to satisfy her sweet tooth, and take a few minutes off her work day.

Larry was notorious for bringing in gorgeous desserts. That's why they always gave him the job.

"I'm not sure of the flavor, but you gotta see it before it's cut. It has red candied poinsettias all over the top. I even took a picture." Hannah moved into Eve's office and showed her the screen.

"Wow. Maybe I should get something like that while Grace is here."

"You should. It would make a great birthday cake."

It would. Eve made a mental note to ask Larry where he shopped. She was turning fifty this year. She'd told everyone she didn't want to celebrate, didn't want to make it a big deal.

But a birthday cake, that she could do. Especially one as pretty as the one waiting for her in the conference room.

"When does Grace get in?"

"Two weeks. Her flight arrives late Saturday night. I plan on spending all day Sunday in our pj's watching movies and catching up. A cake like that will do nicely for our movie marathon."

Eve stood up to follow Hannah out of her office, only to turn back when her phone buzzed on her desk. She saw Grace's name light up. "Hannah, it's my daughter. I'll be there in a second."

She clicked and held the phone up to her ear. "Hey, beautiful, what's up? We were just talking about you."

The line crackled a bit. "Mom? Can you hear me?"

Eve moved to the other side of her office. She leaned against her window, which always seemed to work. "Better?"

Her daughter's voice rang out clear. "Yes. Um, I have something I need to talk to you about."

Eve recognized that voice. The voice that said bad news

was about to come out of her daughter's mouth. "What is it?" She tried to hold the frustration from her voice. She knew this wasn't going to be good.

"You know how I'm working on that side project for my professor?"

"Yes."

"I have a chance to spend a week with a consulting firm the first week in January."

"Honey, that's great news. Congratulations, I'm excited for you."

"Thanks. I'm super excited about it. But I have to be prepared for it. Professor Faulk has given me all kinds of data I need to review before I go. This will be good for my project, and for my resume. Not that I ever thought of working here in Spain, but this would be an ideal job for me out of college. So, I'd love the opportunity to work with them for a week before we start back to school."

Her daughter was rambling. Which meant she needed something, and she was trying to figure out how to ask. She leaned her head against the cool window, closing her eyes.

"Grace, what are you trying to say?"

"Would it be okay if I don't come home? I just don't think I can do it. Not and be prepared the way I want to be for this opportunity. We can FaceTime all Christmas Day. And we can plan a trip next year, when I'm back home. And …"

Eve was stunned. She could hear Grace talking, trying to appease her. But only one thought went through her mind: Not spend the holidays with her only daughter?

Her world closed in, just a bit.

She'd been looking forward to it on so many levels.

Her brother was taking his family to Hawaii for Christmas. With one child in high school and the other a freshman in college, they'd decided this might be the last year they could do it as a small family.

Her mother had died several years before. Her father was seeing someone new, and they'd decided to go skiing in Whistler for Christmas with another couple from their retirement community.

She'd been so happy thinking it would be just the two of them this holiday.

And now, nothing.

Nobody.

Just her. And a big, fucking poinsettia cake she was totally going to get and eat every last bite of while watching all of the holiday movies on Netflix.

She bit her tongue. She counted to five.

She was a mom. She knew what she had to do, no matter how much she wanted to whine.

"Whatever you think is best," Eve finally said through gritted teeth. *This is my mom voice*, she told herself. *Just keep sounding positive.*

"Are you sure?" Grace squeaked out. "Cause I can come home. I hate to think of you all alone."

Eve could hear her daughter's voice move from excitement to worry. And though she totally wanted to be selfish and demand her daughter come home, she knew deep inside she had to give her space. She'd deal with her own feelings later, but for now, she had to squash the worry in Grace's voice once and for all.

"Honey, I'll be fine. You know that."

"You could spend it with Grandpa."

She forgot Dad's in Whistler. "I could. I will."

"And I'm serious about next spring when I get back. We can start planning a trip after the new year. We can spend a week together, before I start to work."

"Of course, we can. We'll have plenty of other Christmases together." And fiftieth birthdays. Grace seemed to have forgotten that too.

"Thanks, Mom. I knew you'd understand."

They made promises to talk later over the weekend. Eve clicked off and dropped her phone to her desk.

She stood looking out at the clouds. It looked gloomier than before.

She had two weeks off. Two weeks! And now she was supposed to sit in her home all by herself, celebrate her fiftieth, Christmas, and New Year's Eve all by herself?

9

What kind of loser had she become?

How had this become her life?

She was fifty, not dead.

She worked out three nights a week. She was vegetarian. The doctor had given her a clean bill of health just two months before.

She felt great. She even looked good. She could still turn a guy's eye when she wanted to. When she and her friends went out.

"Hey, you coming?" Bill poked his head in her office.

Her staff was getting restless. Cake was calling. And since she was one of three birthdays in December, they wouldn't cut it without her.

"Sure." She tucked her phone in her pocket, put on her best smile, and followed Bill down the hall.

She snapped a picture of the cake - it really was a fantastic cake. Maybe she'd still order one all for herself.

She helped cut it into enough pieces for everyone in the office. Then settled back into her office with the biggest piece.

And a great big sugary poinsettia flower to gnaw on later.

"Fuck birthdays. Fuck Christmas," she mumbled to herself. And shoved a great big bite into her mouth.

Eve hung her dripping coat on the peg on the wall. She dropped her bags on the floor on the way to her office. She fell into the chair, opened up her laptop, and waited for it to come to life.

She pulled up Google and started searching, *best cities for Christmas in Spain*. Within a few moments, she narrowed her focus to one place: Mallorca, Spain. It was one of Spain's largest islands located in the middle of the Mediterranean. It was known for its beach resorts, sheltered coves, and limestone mountains. Spain's royal family preferred Mallorca for their own holiday festivities.

That was good enough for her.

She pulled up another browser window and searched for flights. While they were higher than she liked to spend, she considered it a fiftieth birthday present to herself. But before she hit the buy button, she grabbed her mobile and called her daughter instead.

"Mom? Are you okay?" Grace sounded sleepy.

It was only then Eve remembered the time difference. "Oops, sorry honey. I forgot what time it was there."

"You're okay?"

"Yes. Sorry to panic you. But I have an idea."

"Okay."

"What if I come there instead? I just did some research. I could book a room in Mallorca for a week. Could you meet me there for Christmas?"

"Really? I've wanted to go there. Everyone says it's fabulous."

"That's what I've read too. I've got my finger on the buy button for an airplane ticket. Should I do it? Can you meet me?"

"I suppose I could take off a week. And bring some of my research with me."

"Exactly. And we don't have to do touristy things from sunup to sundown. I'll get a room at a resort, and we can hang out by the pool."

"It might not be that warm. It's pretty chilly here right now."

"So, we'll hang out by the pool with blankets. I really want this. It'd be a great birthday present."

"Ohmigod," Grace gasped as she dropped the phone.

Eve could hear her swearing as she picked it back up. "I forgot it's your fiftieth. Mom, I'm so sorry."

Eve rolled her eyes. *Exactly. You forgot it was my birthday.*

And just as quick, her mom voice kicked into gear. *She's got a lot on her plate. I raised a good kid. She would have remembered eventually.*

"No worries."

"Yes. Do it. Come to Spain. I'll make it work. And I promise we'll do something great on your day."

Eve clicked, and her ticket was confirmed. She was going to Spain!

Chapter Two

After twelve hours of flight time, she was finally in Mallorca. Eve breathed in deep as she walked from the plane into the terminal. The flight attendant had said it was unusually warm for this time of year, and it was expected to continue through the holidays.

That worked for her. Maybe they wouldn't need blankets by the pool after all.

The resort she booked had told her they had a shuttle to and from the airport. She could meet her driver by baggage claim. She followed the crowds and found it easily.

After retrieving her suitcases - one for clothes, one for gifts - she pushed and pulled her bags looking for her name. Thirty minutes later, she was ready to drop.

She was a seasoned traveler. She'd traveled the world since she was a little girl. Maybe it was the time of year. But she was having a hard time hiding her frustration, or pushing aside the feeling of wanting to crawl into bed and sleep.

She started pulling her bags to the side, and ran into a man with a sign for her hotel.

Relieved, she pointed to the name at the top. "That's me. That's my hotel."

The man looked dapper in his dark suit and cap. He must have been about her dad's age. He frowned, shaking his head.

She smiled at him, trying again in broken Spanish.

"No." He pointed to the name underneath the logo. *Mayfield.* Definitely not her.

She pulled out a file from her bag and found a paper copy of the receipt she'd printed from the hotel. She gave it to the man, hoping he'd understand.

"See? This is me. I'm going to the hotel too."

He kept shaking his head. Pointing back to his sign, to the name written in dark print. He wouldn't budge.

She took a deep breath. And then another one. She just wanted a ride to the hotel, a nice meal, a chance to see her daughter …

"Hi, I'm Mayfield."

She turned and looked into a gorgeous set of brown eyes. American, she guessed, by his accent. He was a little taller than her. His short brown hair graying at the temples. It curled every which way, giving him that just-out-of-bed look.

She shook her head slightly. He was good looking. But right now, she was hungrier for a sandwich and a bubblebath than good conversation.

"I've been searching for almost an hour for my ride to the same hotel. I'm just not that good at Spanish, but he seems not to have my name on file."

He read over her receipt, then turned it for the driver to see. He broke out in fluent Spanish, going back and forth until they both nodded their heads in agreement.

"Give him a minute. He has to call it in. But he says it shouldn't be a problem to bring us both to the resort. Otherwise, you'd have to wait for the next shuttle, which could be another hour."

There was no way she could stand here with two suitcases for that long. Still, she was caught off guard when he laughed heartily.

"I'm sorry, but your face. Rough flight?"

She shook her head. "Actually, no. But it has been a rough two weeks. All of my holiday plans changed two weeks ago, and my quiet plans with my daughter in Seattle have now turned into me traveling halfway around the world to visit her instead. I'm just," she searched for the right word, gave up and said, "tired."

The driver was nodding his head, looking at the two of them.

Mayfield translated as the driver finished his conversation.

"He says the hotel has you on file, and he'll bring you along too. It looks like you'll be able to relax very soon."

"Oh, thank god. I was ready to just park everything in a

corner and give up for a while. Thanks for your help."

"Sure, not a problem. We Americans have to stick together," he winked. He was traveling light, so he grabbed one of her suitcases and followed the driver out to the curb.

They deposited their bags into the trunk, then settled into the back of the car.

"I'm Shay, by the way. Shay Mayfield." He held out his hand.

She folded her hand into his. "Eve Nichols. Shay Mayfield. Aren't you in Inc Magazine this month?"

A look of surprise crossed his face. He held up his hands. "Guilty as charged."

She thought back to the story she'd read while eating dinner a few nights before. "You created a security platform. Sold it to Google."

"That's me. Living the dream."

"I think that's everyone's dream, selling something to Google."

"I suppose. I didn't start with that thought in mind. But I

can't argue with the outcome." He moved in his seat, turned to face her. "So, tell me, Eve. What do you do? I'm at a distinct disadvantage here since you know about me, and other than your name and knowing you're about to see your daughter, I know nothing about you."

"I'm from Seattle. I work at Shutterbug."

Shutterbug was one of the top royalty-free stock photo houses in the world. She'd started with them fifteen years before, when they were just a startup. She'd started when salaries were low, and stock options flowed freely. Luckily, she'd been smart enough to max out her stock options before it went public. Now she worked more because she didn't know what else to do, rather than having to.

"Great site. I use them all the time for stock photos."

"That's us."

"What do you do for them?"

"I'm in HR. I've worked there for years."

"Do you like Seattle?"

She nodded. "For the most part. I travel a lot. Especially

in the winter and spring. As long as you get out of the rain here and there, it's a great town to live in."

"I agree. I love going up there."

"But you're from Silicon Valley from what I remember, right?"

"Yep. I've been there since college."

"Any kids?" She wanted to add wife to her question, but she held back.

"Nope. My ex works for one of the top law firms. We never seemed to have time to make the kid thing work."

"I get that. My ex and I only had one. After paying as much as we have for college these past three years, I'm kind of glad she's our only."

"You're meeting her here?"

"Yes. Grace is studying here in Spain for her junior year. She got a last-minute chance to work with a consulting firm for a week right after the new year, and she wanted to stay and do her research so she'd be better prepared. I wasn't about to sit home alone, so I booked a flight, made a reservation, and here I am."

She couldn't stop looking at him.

She hadn't dated a lot since her divorce. Enough to know it was difficult finding a really great guy. Enough to know she rarely had an instant connection, not like the energy she felt sitting next to Shay.

"It's just the two of you this week?"

Was he fishing, or was that her imagination?

"It is. All of my family had other plans. And you? Are you here for the week or just a quick business trip?" She envisioned him jet setting all over the world on a whim.

"Nope. Just me. Maybe some site seeing. A hike. Hopefully, without a phone."

"If you hand it to me, I can throw it out the window. You can claim you lost it later."

He gave it to her. She rolled down the window, and made a fake move. Not knowing him well enough, she elected to roll it back up. She smiled as she handed it back to him.

He tucked it into his coat pocket. "I kinda wished you

would have."

"That bad?"

He sighed. "I shouldn't complain. Maybe it's just the time of year."

A frown crossed his face. He watched the passing scenery for a bit before turning back to her. "Sorry. Don't mean to put a damper on things. It's the first year without my ex. Which isn't that bad; we separated almost two years ago."

Then he said softer, "It's also the first Christmas without my mom."

She touched his hand gently. "I'm sorry."

Yeah, she knew how bad that one was. "I lost my mother several years ago to cancer. The first year was awful. I wish I could say it gets easier. It doesn't. They all pretty much suck."

He glanced at her.

She held his eyes, as if sharing their pain.

He nodded. "Cancer, too. She looked so thin those last few weeks. I'm trying not to remember her as that person."

They rode in silence for a few minutes. She watched the

passing cars, the scenery.

It was a beautiful place. She'd been all over Spain, studying abroad herself for a semester way back when.

She used to be fluent. She used to use her Spanish regularly. But now, she was like any of the countless Americans who only pulled a few words out when they headed out on vacation.

She recognized a lot of the signs as they navigated along. She'd picked up on a few concepts as she'd weaved through the airport. But like any muscle that's left unused, her Spanish was more than a little rusty.

Maybe she'd pick it up again as she spent the next few days on the island.

The sun shone high in the sky. She could feel the warmth through the car window.

Without thinking, she said, "You can join us if you'd like. For meals. Whatever you're comfortable with."

He looked a little shocked. But his smile was almost as instant. "Maybe. I'd like that."

"We're here through the weekend."

"Me too."

The car pulled up to the hotel doors. The driver helped them out of the car, and gave their bags to the porter. They walked in together, stood in line, checked in.

She pointed down a hallway. "I'm down here."

He pointed at the elevator. "I'm up."

"It's a small hotel. We're planning on staying fairly close. I'm sure we'll see you."

"Okay."

He didn't move. His eyes never left hers.

She took a step towards him, held out her hand. She really wanted to touch him one more time.

He moved forward, reaching around for a hug.

And somewhere in the middle, her finger got caught in his jacket, her cheek bumped his nose.

They both pulled away looking a little horrified, before bursting into a fit of giggles.

"Sorry."

"Jet lag," he mumbled. Before turning towards the elevator, pulling his bag behind him.

He pushed the button, turned, and grinned. "It was nice meeting you, Eve."

"You too, Shay."

She followed the porter down the hall and glanced back one more time.

He was very good looking. In another time, another place …

Chapter Three

Eve walked around the suite she'd reserved for the week. She'd lucked out, calling just a few moments after another guest had canceled. Like the flight, the suite was a little higher priced than she liked to pay, but she figured just a couple of weeks before Christmas, she couldn't afford to be choosy.

Now she was glad she'd booked.

It had two bedrooms, a living space, and a bathroom she knew both she and Grace would spend a lot of time in. She sighed as she stared at the tub.

Modern chic and elegance enveloped her around every corner. It was classic shades of brown, beige, and white, with a hint of teal thrown in. The beds looked super comfortable. Was it wrong if she wanted to spend the week propped up on a pillow, with a book in hand?

She chose one of the bedrooms and emptied her suitcase into the closet and drawers. Then she returned to the living space with the other, opened it, and pulled out her gifts.

She was happy to see a small tree fully decorated. The desk clerk had responded to Eve's emailed request for the decorations, stating it was not an uncommon request; they'd see to everything. And boy had they delivered.

The tree was classy, matching the decor she'd seen in the lobby. Baubles of green and red danced on each branch, while twinkle lights sparkling in between.

Even the sofa and chairs added to the festivities, with red and green pillows and blankets for snuggling.

She carefully placed all of her gifts for her daughter under the tree, then opened up the curtains and went out onto the deck. Their website assured her she'd have a spectacular view. It hadn't done the view justice.

Sweeping views over the city took her breath away. She could see the Cathedral where they would be spending

Christmas Eve at. The Mediterranean was off in the distance.

And even though it was daylight, she could see the magic of the holidays all around her. Decorated trees were everywhere. She could even hear sleigh bells off in the distance. She left the door open as she went back inside.

She found her phone in the bottom of her bag and texted her daughter. She responded with:

Just landed.

That meant she'd see her in about an hour.

She was in a new city! She could hardly believe she'd thrown this trip together in less than two weeks.

This was way out of her comfort zone. Normally she needed months to plan.

It reminded her of another time and place, before marriage and kids when she'd been more spontaneous. Before life turned her into a planner.

As she took another look around, she decided she was

glad her daughter had chosen to stay in Spain. This was going to be fun.

She glanced at her watch; just enough time to firm up the details for the rest of their trip.

She gathered up her bag filled with brochures, and headed down to the lobby to talk with the concierge.

The lobby was bustling with couples and families in town for the holidays. Furniture had been arranged around a very large tree. Eve guessed it must be at least fifteen feet high, with a beautiful angel perched on top.

And the smell! It even smelled like Christmas, with just the right amount of cinnamon and cloves, like fresh-baked cookies from the oven.

She watched a family with a little girl who stood in awe by the tree. She pointed to teddy bears and little toy drums, with the wonderment only three-year-olds can have. She'd loved when Grace was that age.

The concierge was buy with several in line. She stood and waited, keeping a watchful eye on the door for her daughter.

A young woman not much older than Grace offered to help.

"Hi, when I booked a couple of weeks ago, the agent assured me that when I got here, I could firm up some last-minute sightseeing trips. It's just my daughter and me."

"Of course. Did you have anything in mind?" The woman placed several brochures in front of Eve and told her what to expect. "These companies are for guests only. We make room and can squeeze you into any of them."

"Perfect."

"Do you like wine?"

Eve nodded. "Yes, we both do."

"Then you should try our wineries tour. It's a five-hour tour that goes down into the Binissalem DO region. They'll bring you to two separate wineries, with a stop for lunch in between. It's one of our most popular trips."

With two openings the day before Christmas Eve, she jumped at the chance. She browsed through the other brochures while the woman called in the reservations. She printed out the final tickets and tucked them into a folder.

"That leaves two other days before the Christmas festivities," Eve mused. "I was hoping to book spa time during one of those days. Maybe we could do this Jeep tour tomorrow?"

Eve handed back a brochure to the woman, who nodded and tapped into her computer.

"We do have two openings tomorrow. It holds four, so you may join one other party."

Eve nodded. "That's okay. We love to meet other people."

"Perfect. This tour is about six hours total. You'll leave at ten tomorrow morning. You'll ride up a steep mountain road to Sa Calobra, two of our most stunning beaches. I should warn you; this drive isn't for the faint-hearted. It's full of twists and turns, not a good choice if either of you gets motion sickness."

Eve smiled. "That's not a problem. We'll both be fine." She remembered just a few years before her daughter had taken her to an arcade that was filled with virtual reality. Grace had designed a roller coaster and then made them both get into a cage that simulated it in action. If both of them had survived that, they could handle anything.

"The driver will have a picnic lunch for you to enjoy on one of the beaches. Do you have any dietary restrictions?"

"Could we make both meals vegetarian?"

"Is cheese okay?"

"Yes, that would be fine."

"I'll make a note of it." The woman tapped into the computer, made another call, printed off her reservation form, and tucked it into her folder.

"And I'd like to book spa treatments for the day in between these." Eve picked up the spa brochure again, contemplating her options. She selected facials, massages, and finished it up with skin pampering and makeup sessions.

"Would you like blow-outs too? They can style your hair for an evening on the town."

"Why not?" It was her birthday celebration, after all. She'd thrown a little black dress into her suitcase as an afterthought. "Could you recommend a restaurant too? Something with vegetarian selections?"

"I know just the place." With a sparkle in her eye, she hopped up and disappeared into the back room.

A moment later she came back out, paper in hand. She sat down at the phone, and made a reservation.

"You're going to love this place. They're one of the best on the island. I've made a note you prefer vegetarian. They are quite accommodating." She printed off another sheet with reservations, and tucked it into her folder.

"Is that all I can do for you?"

Eve smiled. "Thank you so much for your help. You've just ensured we'll have a great time."

"Glad to help!"

As Eve was walking back into the lobby, she heard a squeal from behind.

"Mom!"

Her daughter nearly tackled her with a hug.

Eve breathed her in. She smelled like coffee and fresh

air. She pulled her tighter, etching it in her memory for later.

"Did you just get here?"

"I did. I'm so glad you're here!"

The two walked arm and arm back down the hall, pulling her luggage behind them.

Grace told her mom all about her flight.

Eve told her daughter all about their travel plans for the next few days.

As she threw open the door to the suite, Grace let out another squeal. "No way! It's gorgeous in here."

Grace ran straight for tree, touching the ornaments one by one. She picked up one of the gifts, shook it gently, before looking wide-eyed at her mom, "Are these for me?"

Eve crossed over to the tree, gently tapped her on the head. "Of course, they are, silly girl. Don't you know you're my one and only?"

Grace stood, hugging her mom.

Eve felt a happy sigh settle in. She felt complete, once again. Just like she always did whenever her daughter was near.

"Hey, you only turn fifty once."

Grace jumped back, crossed over to her luggage.

"Speaking of fifty, I have a gift for you."

"You didn't have to do that."

"Of course, I did."

Grace opened up her suitcase and pulled out jeans, t-shirts, and shoes. There, tucked in a pair of socks, was a small red box. She handed it to her mom.

"I hope you like it."

"I already love it."

She unwrapped it and found a delicate chain necklace with a wire wrapped pendant. In the center was a rose quartz stone, a beautiful shade of pink, Eve's favorite color.

Grace took it and put it around her mother's neck. "A woman makes these not far from the school. She told me this stone represents unconditional love. She said it gives energy for inner peace and calm. It helps you find your way in the world, through love and focus. It helps you accept new things while giving you strength to move forward. That sounded like you.

That's everything we've talked about this past year. It's everything I want to give you for your fiftieth."

Eve was speechless. She knew she'd cry if she said a word. She walked over to a mirror and fingered it around her neck, looking at the stone and the artistry.

When had her daughter gotten so smart?

When had her daughter gotten so tall! She'd come in from behind and wrapped her arms around. Standing there, Eve went back and forth between her new necklace and her daughter's eyes.

If everything else in her life was a little up in the air at the moment, it was nice to know she'd done one thing right.

Chapter Four

Eve and Grace settled into a booth at the restaurant and ordered a bottle of wine.

Eve hadn't been able to get a word in edgewise since she'd met up with her daughter, and she wouldn't have it any other way.

She missed that most.

It had been just the two of them as Grace had finished high school. They'd made it a habit of sitting down for dinner most nights of the week.

Often, their conversations would stretch several hours, diving into all kinds of topics. They'd tried to continue it as Grace entered college. The shared dinner at least once a week through FaceTime, and shared everything from what books they were reading to the latest topic in the news.

Now watching her daughter, she knew that's what she missed the most with her being overseas. Time difference between Spain and Seattle weren't conducive to trying to connect for several hours. They relied more on email and texting than speaking.

The waiter popped the cork on their selection, before letting Eve take the first sip. When she approved, he poured two glasses and set them in front of them. She ordered an appetizer and sat back, ready to relax.

"Tell me all about this job you had to stay in Spain for." Eve had been so busy making reservations and finishing up at work for the year; she never got the chance to find out more about what was holding her daughter here.

Grace picked up the napkin, unrolled the silverware from within. She placed the knife, fork, and spoon on the table, before placing the fabric in her lap. "It's not a job per se. But I've told you about Dr Faulk's class and how I'm helping him on the side."

"Yes. You've loved his class."

"I do. He's given me so many ideas on where to look for a job when I graduate."

"And that's where you think this *job* will help you?"

Grace picked up her wine glass, swirled the liquid around. She rolled her head to the side in a familiar way, the one that said she was choosing her words carefully, the one that Eve had forgotten how much she missed.

"There's a company I've had my eye on for the past few months, ever since I got here and started doing research. Robbins Consulting Group has a global presence in social impact consulting. They have offices in New York and San Francisco, as well as Barcelona, Paris, Berlin, Sydney, Rio. Others too, but you get it; they're big."

Grace moved forward in her seat, her eyes glowed with anticipation. Her hands darting around as she spoke.

Eve absentmindedly reached over, moving Grace's wine glass just out of reach.

Grace continued, "Anyway, they work with governments

and businesses to change the world through global development, global health, environmental impact, and they even have an impact investing department. They go in and work with developing nations to help change the world. They're having a symposium the first week of January, kind of a kick-off to start the year out right, and it's going to be here in Spain, up in Barcelona. People are coming from all of the offices, and they invited several professors to bring along teams as well. Dr Faulk nominated six of us, and we're all traveling together to attend."

"It's part of your school tuition? Do I need to pay for air or hotel?"

"Yes, but it's reasonable. They booked tickets through the department, and we're going to be staying in a dorm. So the cost is very minimal. I didn't run it by you because it happened so fast. But it is just a few hundred dollars."

"That's not a problem. Did you charge it?"

"I did."

"Okay. I'll pay it when I'm back home. What will you be learning? What will you be doing?"

"They have different learning programs for students. They do this frequently, I guess. Plus, they're also going to let us sit in on meetings so we can see planning processes, education opportunities, and other strategy sessions to see how this industry works."

"Is there intern potential by going to this?"

Grace nodded her head as she sipped. "That's the best thing. This company has a variety of internships. I've already started the application process. I can put in for as many offices as I'm willing to work at this next summer. And Dr Faulk will write a recommendation, so I think that gives me an even better chance."

"That sounds good to me. What location are you thinking of putting in for?"

Eve almost laughed. She knew even without asking, her daughter was planning on using this as a way to travel more. She could see it in her face.

Grace had been enamored with traveling ever since their trip to Paris when she was in third grade. The view from the top of the Eiffel Tower had stuck with her throughout the years, it was the one thing she spoke of most often.

Grace had traveled to Washington DC for an eight grad field trip, flown to London for a high school choir expedition. And even before she'd settled on a college, she'd started planning her study abroad program.

Eve knew Grace would always be a world traveler, and that was find with her. Yet the little girl in her now held back from telling Eve just where she wanted to go.

"I take it you're applying to stay here in Europe."

"Would that be bad?" Grace eyed her sheepishly.

"Are you even thinking of applying for the U.S. offices?"

"Definitely. They have a huge US presence. But I wanted to put in for several more too. I figure that'll give me more of a shot of being hired."

"Is there a way to put in for all of them? To increase your odds?"

Eve almost laughed as she watched the shock cross her

daughter's eyes.

"Grace, I know how much this means to you. You've just told me this is a key player in the industry, right?"

"Yes."

"And an internship would look great on your resume. Possibly even lead to a job."

"Yes."

"So, getting the internship would be a very good thing."

"It would. I really want it."

"Then why don't you put in for all of it? For any opportunity in any country? It'll only be for what, ten, twelve weeks?"

"It's a ten-week program."

"I think you could handle ten weeks anywhere, couldn't you? And I'm assuming they help their interns with housing, or at least a point in the right direction?"

"Yes. Dr Faulk has all kinds of resources. I even checked in with my advisor back home. She sent me some things that she has for this internship too."

"Then, just do it. What can I do to help?"

Grace squealed, jumped up, and hugged her mom, before dropping back into her seat. "I knew this was going to be a good opportunity coming to Spain. But I had no idea it would lead to all of this!"

Even smiled. "Sometimes things happen because they're meant to be. How many times have I told you that?"

The waiter placed their appetizer in front of them. They nibbled while Grace walked her through the classes she'd had the previous three months.

She loved watching her daughter so filled with life, so excited. Telling her in detail about the teachers, the students, and what she was learning.

Grace was ready to take on the world in a big way. Eve saw that, and it made her proud. She was happy she'd raised a thoughtful, considerate, and passionate child.

But there was something more, an inkling way deep down inside of her gut.

I remember that feeling.

The thought hit her out of nowhere.

She remembered how sure she felt coming out of college. She was going to find the job of her dreams; she'd known it.

Of course, she'd had a bigger desire to find a man.

No matter how much the world had told her generation that women could do anything, there was always an underlying belief they could only have it if a man was waiting in the wings, supporting them.

She'd come out of college without a man. It had taken her three years of working and living on her own before she found someone worthy to slip a ring on her finger. And even with that, she'd made the wrong choice.

To be fair, he'd been a good guy for a long time. They just stopped clicking after a while. They didn't want the same things out of life. Clearly, what her ex had wanted was something younger. It still drove her crazy as his girlfriends continued to get closer and closer to their daughter's age.

But that was his life. She had hers.

The problem now was she wasn't quite sure what she wanted.

She was free for the first time in her life to do anything she pleased. She had enough stock options she could retire and start doing something else.

She'd downsized two years before, selling off the big family home and moving to a condo closer to work.

She was as healthy as she had been out of college. Her recent doctor's visit confirmed she was *normal* on every level. No prescriptions for her. She worked hard for it, and she was glad it was paying off.

She could do anything a healthy fifty-year-old would want to do.

The trouble was, she had no idea what that was.

Open a business? She'd dreamed about it for years, but nothing ever seemed right. And it was a lot of work if she just wasn't sure.

Start up a charity? Again, too much work.

But she didn't just want to sail off into the sunset. She

had a lot of ambition. The trouble was, she didn't have something calling out to her: pick me, pick me.

She liked traveling.

She liked photography.

She liked working with people.

But how did you combine all that into something more? She wasn't about to start over at the bottom. She was the director of her department, and she wasn't going down. Not unless she started something herself.

Maybe she could start up a food company. Or go back to culinary school. She loved cooking, when she had the time.

"Mom?"

"Hmmm?" What did she miss? Maybe she could blame it on jet lag.

"You okay?"

"I'm fine. Maybe a little tired."

"You want to order?" Grace pointed to the waiter standing to her left.

"Oh, yes. Of course." She glanced down at the menu,

trying to remember what she'd decided on. She pointed to an entree and handed the menu back to the waiter.

"How's work going?"

"Fine. You know how it is this time of year. Not much is happening in the office. I'm glad to have two weeks off."

"How's grandpa?"

"He's good. I told you he's in Canada skiing, didn't I? He and Joann went with friends."

"You did. I talked with him two days ago to wish him Merry Christmas. It sounded like they were having a blast."

"I think they are. They seemed excited to go."

"You sure you're okay?" Grace sat observing Eve, eyes squinted, pondering her mom's actions. "Is fifty getting to you?"

That caught Eve off guard. "What? No. Why?"

"I don't know. You seem like you're …" Grace waved her hand back and forth, trying to find the right words.

Yep, that described her perfectly. Even her daughter couldn't put a finger on it.

She wanted something. What the hell was it?

Chapter Five

Eve huffed out of her room, almost running into another couple coming down the hall.

"Excuse me."

She slowed, trying to calm down.

How could she have assumed this would be a girl's trip? That her daughter might just want to spend time with her? Her thoughts were ugly, and she knew it.

Still, she was pissed.

She'd flown all the way from Seattle, and the first day into their holiday together was going to have her spending the day alone.

Grace had told her she needed to be close to her phone. Her instructor was going to call her with more information on her weeklong research project.

Just as adamantly, Eve told her she wanted to go on this tour. And she did. She had always been adventurous. Hiking was something you did when you lived in the Pacific Northwest.

She'd seen pictures of the view from the beaches. And a Jeep tour was just what she needed to have a little fun. Why wasn't her daughter equally excited?

She was doing this, no matter what. If her daughter wanted to sit in the room all day, fine by her. They didn't need to do everything together.

She made her way to the front lobby, where she'd been instructed to meet her driver. She paced by the window, looking out at the sun filtering in from behind the trees.

"Beautiful weather, isn't it?"

She turned around to see the same pair of gorgeous eyes she'd spent time with the day before. "Shay."

"Eve."

"Good to see you again." She couldn't resist the urge to hug him.

She breathed deep; the same aftershave he'd had on in the taxi, only stronger. Better.

His wild hair was even a bit wilder, with curls going this way and that.

A quick flick of her eyes noticed he had on well-worn jeans that hugged him in all the right places.

Yep, he did things to her insides.

"You were the one who said it was a small hotel. I guess this proves it." He looked at her mischievously. "Is your daughter around?"

And the frown returned. "It seems we're splitting up today. She has to wait for a phone call, so I'm doing a tour by myself."

"Any chance you're hopping in a Jeep to check out a couple of beaches?"

"How'd you - " she stopped mid-sentence. "You're going too."

He grinned. "Sounds like fun, doesn't it?"

She nodded. "It does, actually. That's why I told my

daughter I was going with or without her."

"Good for you. Now we can spend the day together."

Why was she suddenly glad her daughter had chosen to stay in the room?

The driver approached, asking for their paperwork. She explained how her daughter was staying behind. When he had both of their confirmations, he asked them to follow him outside.

"It's just the two of us?"

"Yes," the driver confirmed.

She was met by another grin from Shay.

"Did you plan this?" She gave him a playful look.

"Maybe," he teased. "Is there anything wrong with that?"

"Not at all!"

She slid in behind the driver and buckled in.

He sat down beside her.

In minutes, they were on the road to Sa Calobra, with their driver explaining the history as they drove.

"Sa Calobra was just a small seaside village. When they connected the road, the designers decided to make the road as much a destination as the village itself. Today it's one of the most magical roads in the world."

The rock formations were nothing short of spectacular. Olive trees popped up all around them. Grasses popped in and out of the rocks.

And the drive was even better.

Eve was glad she'd opted for a driver rather than renting a car. The road gave a new meaning to the word *hairpin turns*. More than once, she ducked, thoroughly convinced they were about to hit a rock. And each time, the driver laughed and continued on their journey.

He stopped when he could, allowing them to get out and photograph the browns and greens of the terrain against the blues of the Mediterranean and the sky. She kept her phone busy, shooting in every direction.

She was also glad she'd opted to bring along a big bottle of sunscreen, and a hat to keep the sun off her face. After a

53

couple of hours with the sun beating down on her, she was ready for a break.

They stopped at a secluded beach, parked, and found a table in the shade to enjoy a picnic lunch. Their driver set the table, then disappeared to enjoy his own lunch.

"Have you been here before?" She'd just shared one of the best drives of her life with a man she knew little about. And yet somehow, she felt she knew him well after ducking into his shoulder more than once.

He'd been a good sport about it, laughing as she squealed. She enjoyed it when he wrapped his arm around her shoulders and held her protectively. Maybe she'd done it more for the feeling than out of fear? She wasn't sure, but she didn't care.

"No. You?"

"Nope. I've been to Spain several times. I was here for a semester in college years ago. But I've never visited any of the islands before now."

"Did your daughter pick this place?"

She shook her head. "When she changed her mind and couldn't come home, I happened upon this place by chance. I was looking for Christmas holidays close to her school, and I saw this island mentioned several times."

"I had a friend recommend it. I was looking for an escape. Something that would keep me busy during the days. This fit the bill."

"I would imagine the hiking is phenomenal."

"Do you like to hike?"

"Love it. The Pacific Northwest is the best."

"It is pretty. I've spent quite a bit of time up in Seattle. Everyone thinks Silicon Valley is where it's at, but I know Seattle is giving it a run for its money."

They unpacked the picnic basket their driver had left on the table. Sandwiches, salad, and drinks for both.

"I know you sold your business to Google last year. What are you doing now?"

"Retired?" He said without conviction. "Or maybe I should say looking for another business. I'm not sure at this point. Technically, I don't run anything. But I sit on a couple of startup boards. I have a lot of friends creating new internet businesses. I help out when I can."

"That sounds fun. You get to do what you want, when you want."

He nodded. "Something like that. It sounds a lot better than it is."

"Don't like retirement much?"

"Is retirement even a thing anymore?"

She thought about that for a moment. It was a long way off in her mind, and she could tell he was about her age. "So, you're still young enough to want to do something. You're just not sure what that looks like."

"Exactly! Not at my age, anyway. I'm just not sure what I want to do next."

"Do you have any plans?"

"I dunno. Maybe? I know that sounds like a crazy answer, but it's been a difficult year."

"I get that. I can't imagine going through a divorce,

dealing with the death of your mom, plus selling a company all at the same time."

"When you put it that way, it does sound overwhelming."

"Work. Is that all we're going to talk about?"

He snorted. "That seems to be all I do. Even now, I'm always with a friend, answering a question, giving a keynote, or being interviewed. I guess it comes with the territory."

"Do you love it?"

"You mean, what I do now?"

"Yeah. You don't have a business to run anymore. Are you enjoying what you do?"

That stopped him. He ate a couple of bites of his sandwich, thinking. "I've never really thought about it much before."

"That's funny, because that's all I think about these days." She sat straighter, pulled her legs up to her chest, and wrapped her arms around. "I have a big birthday this year, and I've been thinking about what I want to do now. My daughter's doing her own thing. It's just me. I've worked for the same company for fifteen years. It's just all so …" she thought for a minute. "Expected. Boring."

"A big birthday?"

He'd caught that, did he?

"Yep. My fiftieth is on the twenty-fourth."

He nodded, that a-ha moment folding his eyes. "Is that where Eve comes from?"

She ran a hand through her hair, rolled her eyes. "Yeah, I used to think that was my parents' idea of bad humor. Who names their daughter Eve when she's born on Christmas Eve?"

"I think it's clever."

"That's because you didn't grow up teased."

"Really? You don't think Shay is strange? Yes, that's my real name. And when you mix that in with Mayfield, kids came up with all kinds of things. Shay plus M, everyone made shame jokes. I was known as Shamey on my baseball team."

"Oh." She held her hand up to her mouth, stifling a laugh.

"Go ahead. Laugh. I can take it now." He grinned. "In truth, I probably deserved it because I wasn't that good. It was a no-cut sport at my school."

"Computer nerd?"

"Most definitely."

She tried to see him as a computer nerd. In her eyes, he didn't meet any of the qualifications. Not with his classic good looks.

Or maybe it was because she was into nerds herself. Maybe she'd been in the tech industry too long *not* to have a thing for tech guys.

"What do you do for fun in Seattle?"

She thought for a moment, refocused. Then snorted, "Now there's a thought. I work all the time. At least more since my daughter moved to college."

She thought about the last summer. "My dad lives in Seattle too. We love doing wineries together. He loves to kayak, so we do that a lot on the weekends."

His face lit up. "I love kayaking. I can't say I do it all that much. But I did do a week in the San Juan's a few years ago and fell in love with it. Maybe I'll do that again someday."

She nodded. "Yes, do it. That's like my go-to vacation. If I want to escape it all, I'll take a day off, and go for a long weekend. Friday Harbor is my favorite. And there are some great Airbnb's there these days."

"Friday Harbor, eh? You're like the third person that's recommended it to me. I guess I'll have to move it up on my bucket list."

"You won't regret it." She popped the last bite of her sandwich into her mouth.

They packed up their picnic supplies and placed everything back in the basket. They started walking back as their driver hurried over.

"I'm so sorry. I must have hit something in the road on

the way down. The tire is flat. I'm waiting for it to be fixed before we return. But it's not so easy to get repair work done out here. I'm afraid we'll be here for a couple of hours. I apologize." He looked at the two nervously, gauging their response. "We'll be a couple of hours getting back. Do you need to call anyone? I can radio to the hotel."

"I should let my daughter know. She's in my room." In truth, she didn't mind an extra couple of hours sitting on a beach. It was the perfect temperature. And the views were to die for.

"I'll take care of it. I'll let the hotel know." The driver scratched a note onto a pad of paper in his hand.

"I'm fine. It's just me." Shay looked like he had a plan. "We have a couple of hours?"

"Yes. About two. Maybe a little longer."

"I noticed we could hike back up here into the hills. Could we do that and meet back here in two hours?"

The driver nodded, seemingly more pleased they'd have something to occupy their time.

Shay turned to her. "That is, as long as you'd like to join me? We might get better views up there."

She glanced upwards, noticing for the first time a small trail overhead. A few people were making their way up it.

The driver ran back to the car and returned with several more bottles of water.

Shay tucked them into the backpack he'd brought along. "Shall we?" He pointed to the marked trail.

"Why not?"

They hiked in comfortable silence for the first thirty minutes. Eve regularly hiked at home. But the sun and surf were different than in the Pacific Northwest. She was glad the driver had extra provisions they could take along. They each drained a bottle before they reached the first lookout.

They stopped and took in the view.

"It's stunning up here."

"Look, you can see the beach down below."

"Oh, wow, look at the birds."

They took turns pointing in all directions. Eve had her

phone out, capturing all she could.

"You work for a stock photo company, and all you brought was a phone?" He teased.

"Sometimes you just get sick of taking work with you."

"Don't I know it," he whispered almost to himself.

"Says the man who no longer has a company to work for."

"True. But somehow, that doesn't make me any less busy. That's partially why I'm here." He held up his phone. "See? No service?"

"I noticed that. I hope we don't have trouble. We'll never connect with the driver."

He shrugged his shoulders, dismissing the thought of a potential problem. "This is a well-used trail. I scoped them all out online before this trip. I didn't think I'd get a chance to hike it. This is kind of an unexpected surprise."

"Do you hike a lot?" She was curious about him.

"Not as much as I'd like. Of course, maybe now with my newfound freedom, that will change."

He grabbed two bottles of water from his pack, handed one to Eve, and starting joined her on the trail.

Chapter Six

"How did you get into security?" Eve stopped in the small amount of shade just off the path to catch her breath. They were going at a pretty fast pace, and she'd worn too many layers. She pulled her sweatshirt over her head and tied it around her waist.

He moved in closer, ducked down to shield his face from the sun. He opened up a water bottle and took a swig. He handed another bottle to Eve.

"I just fell into it by accident. I had a mathematics degree and found myself working for a software company. I befriended a guy several years older than me who was building a security team and asked me to be a part of it. The rest, as they say, is history."

"What made you go out on your own?"

"I guess that was always my dream. I was the kid with the lemonade stand at seven who actually did very well. My mom told me she wouldn't buy me a new bike, but I could have one if I earned the money. So, I did. In one week."

Eve laughed. "One week?"

Shay grinned. "Yep. Mom challenged me like that a lot after that. She says she saw my potential. And I was always up for a good challenge."

"She sounds like an incredible woman."

"She was."

"Luckily, I put away a lot of cash when I worked for the software company. And I had several people on staff who were really good at getting angel investors. We never had trouble making payroll. It helped a lot those first few years of putting together our platform."

"How long did you build before you sold your first company?"

"Five years. I lived frugally. It worked."

"Are you still friends with the people you started it

with?"

"The guy that built the original security team with the software company I worked for? He became the CIO for my first company. He's been one of my go-to guys for every project I've developed. He's semi-retired now too, but we still kick around ideas from time to time."

"How many companies have you built?"

"Several, but they've all been spinoffs off the original idea. The first business provided the protection needed to secure cloud-based applications. We've refined the technology several times for other industries. Healthcare, for example, takes an entirely different approach to security. It needs added protection because of government regulations. It was more difficult to crack. And then we tapped into the education marketplace. And finally, into the financial platform. They are all slightly different enough that it takes extra thought to protect it from outside influences."

He dove into a few details about performance and development. Eve asked questions about the process, but admitted she knew very little about security.

"I guess you could say I'm probably one who will eventually be a statistic. I use passwords that are far too easy. I'm slow at updating my apps. And I share information about myself that probably leaves me open to hackers everywhere. I know it, and yet I still do it. Is that crazy?"

"No. Not at all. Unfortunately, you're not alone."

"I always swear I'm going to change. But there are only twenty-four hours in the day."

"Until you get hacked. And then you'll spend days in recovery mode."

"Shhh, don't jinx me." She put her hands up to her ears and shook her head. "I have it on my to-do list for the new year if that's any consolation. I'm going to a security class the second week in January with my team members as a part of our annual security training, so I'm planning on making improvements to both my professional and personal security by the end of the month."

"That's a start in the right direction."

"Are you as diligent with your own security? With your laptop and phone?" She nodded her head at the iPhone he held in his hand.

"Probably," he rolled off his tongue, then grinned. "Even I get lazy about things from time to time. But I'd say I'm better than most."

"That's a start." She bumped him with her shoulder, teasing.

He roared with laughter. "Sorry. If you get me started on security, I can talk your ear off."

"I can tell you're passionate about it."

Watching him, she didn't mind at all. His eyes lit up as he spoke. He became more animated. It was a good look on him.

They continued down the trail, walked a few minutes in silence. He moved behind her as another couple navigated beside them, back down the hill, then moved beside her once again.

"You're in HR, you said?"

"Uh, huh. I'm the Director."

"How many employees does Shutterbug have?"

"As of a few days ago, we have four-hundred-twenty-six. We grew by over twenty-five percent last year." It was a statistic she was proud of.

"That must keep you busy."

"Yeah, but I have a good team. We've been growing steadily since I took the job, so we have systems in place."

"Can't argue with success."

"Nope."

"Are you happy there?"

She stopped a moment, and paused.

Several gulls were flying, circling overhead. Their distinctive calling echoed in the distance.

This was the question she'd been contemplating all year.

She had a good life. Everything went according to plan. She got the degree, got the husband, the family, the house, the career. All of it fell into place.

Then she divorced the husband, sold the forever home. The daughter went off to college, and now she was left with a career that was just a job. It didn't fill her with passion. She knew she'd jump at the chance of something that lit her up. But what? What was that? And how was she supposed to know what to do?

Did he really want to know all that?

Still, he asked. And watching him watch her, she suddenly had the feeling he would know better than anyone this feeling inside of wanting more. He'd jumped at opportunities throughout his career.

Maybe he was exactly the right one to ask.

"Can I say: I don't know?"

He looked at her, puzzled.

She kept talking. "I'm good at what I do. I know this company, this industry like the back of my hand. I started when we had less than fifty employees, and moved up rapidly to the head of my department. I've put in a lot of overtime building up our policies and getting our systems in order. I have good people underneath me, and the CEO is flexible with how I grow my department. I've always built strategically, ensuring fifty-hour

71

weeks is the exception, not the norm. I refuse to let anyone get burned out."

"I'm sensing a *but* there."

She nodded. "But after fifteen years, maybe *I'm* burnt out. Or in need of a change. Or maybe … "

"Or maybe it's a combination with that big birthday you're facing." It was his turn to bump her shoulder. He grinned.

"Maybe it is. I don't like to think I'm having a midlife crisis. And really, I enjoy my life. I have everything I could ask for. A great daughter. A job that's given me financial security. I travel when I want. I live in the heart of Seattle and am busy almost every night. I have a great life. But …"

He picked up where she left off. "But maybe it's time for more."

She nodded. "I keep telling myself that. But I have no idea what."

"If you're thinking it, you must have some idea of what you want to do."

She nodded. "Maybe," her voice trailed off. She wasn't sure if she was ready to release her ideas to anyone.

"I sold my latest company just a few months ago. I'm still on board as a consultant, as needed. But the last few weeks, that's getting less and less. I haven't heard anything from them in a week, though part of that may be the holidays. That's one of the reasons I'm here this week. I'm relaxing. I'm thinking about my future. I'm weighing my options. I have a few things I'm interested in, but I don't have to jump quickly at any one thing. I'm exploring. When is the last time you've explored any of your ideas?"

He had her there.

She tried to think of the last time she allowed herself to do anything but work or things for her family. Outside of a bubblebath, she couldn't think of anything.

"I think that's the one thing we get all wrong. I think companies should push sabbaticals much more than they do. The ideas people can come up with when they separate from their regular lives are outstanding. But when you do the same

73

things over and over, you lose yourself."

Is that what was wrong?

She'd been thinking about doing something else for months.

She had a healthy retirement account set up. Her future was secure, thanks to her early stock options.

She'd even toyed around with business ideas, wanting to start something she could be proud of in the coming years.

Maybe even have something that allowed her a little more freedom to travel, especially if her daughter found a job somewhere overseas.

She wanted flexibility.

She wanted something that made her feel good again. Something she could sink her teeth into.

She'd had fun building up her department. But it had been a lot more exciting when it was all brand new. Maybe that's what she missed the most.

Maybe that's what she needed right now.

Something that could set her world on fire once again.

CHRISTMAS EVE

Chapter Seven

"Ohmigod!" Eve reached the summit before Shay. "Look at how blue the water is."

"This is incredible." He pulled his phone from his pocket and took a few photos.

She beat him to it. She was walking to the edge, finding a new perspective, and capturing the view from different angles.

"Look at the boats off in the distance."

"Look at that one!"

"You can see the town, over there."

"I think that's a winery. See the layers on the hill?"

He smiled. "Thanks for doing this with me."

She smiled back. "I can't think of a better way to spend the day."

He glanced at the time on his phone. "That only took us an hour. Want to sit for a bit? It'll be less time going back down."

They found a rock and settled in. She thumbed through her images, showing him the best.

He pulled his photos up and shared.

She might have been aware her leg brushed against his. When was the last time she felt this comfortable with a man?

She hadn't dated in ages. She'd had dinner with someone she'd met at a training class two months before. But she'd turned him down when he asked for date number two.

She believed in magic. She wanted to feel something for someone before she dedicated more than a night on the town.

Not that she was dating Shay. That wasn't happening. They were just here, together. Same place, same time. Sharing a tour together.

But her emotions were playing with her, confusing her. How had he snuck into her thoughts like that?

She liked him. He seemed like a really good guy.

And they ran in the same circles. Two techies from the west coast. She knew that automatically made him more attractive to her. She kinda had a thing for tech guys.

But she couldn't let her emotions run away from her. She was here for Christmas. For her daughter.

And anyway, he was here to recover. To relax. He'd said so.

This was just a fun way to spend the day. *So just put those thoughts away.*

Still, it was a holiday. The weather was perfect. She loved the way the sun felt on her skin. And the way she looked.

She was happy she'd thrown her leggings and tank top into the suitcase at the last minute. She knew she looked good.

Was it wrong she was thinking this way?

He jumped up, brushed the dirt off his pants. He turned to her, offered her a hand. "We need one more picture."

She took his hand, enjoying his touch. "We do?"

"Yep." He led her just off the trail, to a place where the view was the most impressive.

"I'm sure we've shot from here." She started to pull out her phone, but he stopped her.

He snaked an arm around her waist, pulling her into his side. He glanced down. "I think we need a selfie, to remember this by."

"We do." She half-whispered it, dazzled by his touch.

"Is that okay?" He waited for her response.

"Of course." Then she grinned up at him. "Only if you text me a copy."

"Is that a ploy to get my number?"

"Would it work?"

"Definitely."

Hmmm.

Maybe she wasn't the only one thinking about what was happening between them.

She wrapped her arm around his waist. She leaned in, her cheek resting in the crook of his neck.

She hadn't been this aware of a guy in a very long time. It left her tingly all over, acutely aware of everything they were doing.

She watched him touch the screen of his phone, adjust the camera to see their faces, hold it up, and adjust it for the right view.

She couldn't keep from staring at the screen. Her. Him. Right there, looking like they belonged together.

She was nervous, just a little. In all the right ways. Waiting for what came next. Wanting there to be more. Wondering what all this meant.

She matched his grin, hamming it up for the camera.

Then he clicked it off, tucked it into his pocket, and just as quickly stepped in front of her.

His hands were alongside her face before she even knew what to think. Softly settling in like they belonged there. Tenderly holding her, as if this was the most natural thing in the world for them.

She had her sunglasses on, cursed the fact he did too. She couldn't see his eyes, what he was thinking, what they were saying to her. She wanted to read them, find out if he knew what this was all about.

It wasn't just her, or they wouldn't be three inches from one another. He wouldn't be standing there with a question on his mind.

"May I?" Nodding towards her lips.

She didn't take the time to answer with words.

It was the most expected and unexpected thing to happen to her. Possibly ever. And damn if it didn't melt her from the inside out. She gripped his chest as if her life depended on it.

And in some ways, it did. She felt weak, light-headed. She felt as if the stars aligned just for them.

She felt like she was standing in the middle of a romance novel, and the most wonderful, natural thing in the world just happened, just for them.

She didn't feel the wind whipping their hair into each other's faces.

She didn't hear two hikers passing by.

She didn't listen to the birds off in the distance. Or the sound of cars down in the valley.

All she felt was the lips of a man who could kiss like he'd been classically trained.

He pulled apart just enough to say, "This is crazy."

"Completely." She dove right back in.

Time seemed to stand still. Nothing else existed, but his tongue doing wild and crazy things to hers. And even though it was just a kiss, she felt the zing in far-reaching places of her body.

"I think we should start back down," he whispered as he pulled apart.

She was only a little aware of another couple standing near them. She let her eyes flutter, memorizing this feeling. She wanted to relish in it later when she was in the comfort of her own bed.

One final kiss to her forehead brought her back down to earth. "What time is it?"

He brought his phone out of his pocket. "Oh, shit." He leaned over and picked up his pack, grabbed her hand, and headed for the trail. "We have thirty minutes to make it down."

She kept a hold of his hand as they jogged back down the hill.

What was that up there? She couldn't quit asking herself the question.

And even now, why couldn't they let go of one another? It was as if they stopped touching, the connection would break.

Then what?

Then what, indeed.

Right after Grace had left for college, Eve put a little more effort into dating. She'd dated enough to know that it was hard to find someone with similar thoughts, similar passions.

She didn't use Match or Tinder. She wasn't really into the whole swipe thing. Instead, she found guys the old-fashioned way. She got out there and did a lot in the community.

She'd joined a gym. She kayaked on the weekend. She joined several meetup groups that had her busy several nights a month.

She'd even gone on several blind dates through friends of a friend.

She was still friends with several of them. But nothing had materialized any further than just a few dates, a chance to see restaurants and movies with a friendly face.

She didn't want to have sex with a stranger, no matter how much her brain told her she wanted to have sex.

Maybe that was the old-fashioned-ness in her. Her mom had pounded it into her to be a good girl; it still rang true today. She admired that about the younger generation in some ways; they had fewer hangups about what being a good girl meant.

She was almost fifty.

Fifty!

Maybe she deserved to put her good-girl ways to the side.

But how would she do that and find herself in the process?

Or was that part of the process?

Someone new in her life would mean she had a new life. And that might lead to, well, a new life.

Shay came to a stop, and she ran smack into his back

with an "oomph."

He turned around with a grin. "We made it down in twenty. I don't even think the driver's back yet."

She looked around. Sure enough, his car was nowhere to be seen.

Screw the good girl.

She turned and faced him. Wrapped her arms around his neck. Locked eyes with him as she flicked her tongue over his upper lip. She kissed her way over to his neck, nibbled on his ear.

He didn't hold back. His arms wrapped around her waist, pulling her in.

How did this happen? It doesn't make sense, does it?

"No. Not really."

She pulled back, eyebrows up. "Did I say that out loud?"

He grinned. "Would you care to join me tonight for dinner?"

"Yes." She might have said it a little too fast before she remembered. "Um …"

"Your daughter."

"Yeah. I haven't seen her all day." *Which was her own fault. But if she had come, this wouldn't have happened.*

"She's the reason I came to Spain." She was having trouble coming up with reasons why he shouldn't join them.

"I get it." He kissed her lips lightly. "Maybe some other night."

Suddenly, she knew she didn't want to turn him away. She wanted to have dinner with him, maybe see him more throughout their time here on the island. "We'd have to be good. None of this stuff," she leaned in and kissed him.

"But that's the best part." He nibbled her neck.

"There is no way I'm explaining this to my daughter."

"I can be good. We'll just say we had a fantastic time and wanted to continue it."

She nodded. "Okay. But I want to clean up first, so it'll be a bit."

"I have a reservation in the hotel restaurant. I made it for seven, knowing we'd be later because of this tour. I'm sure they can add a couple of place settings."

"Okay."

They heard the driver pull into the parking lot. With one last kiss, they made their way back to the car, crawled in, and buckled up for the ride back.

Chapter Eight

Eve opened up the door to her hotel room and shouted, "Hello?"

No answer.

She texted a quick *where are you*, before heading in for a shower, picking out a dress for the evening on her way there. With no answer from her daughter, she ducked under the water, taking the time to condition her hair.

She toweled off and rechecked her phone. No answer.

She spent a few moments putting on makeup and styling her hair. As she was adding a last coat of mascara, she heard the familiar buzz of her phone.

Met up with friends. Wanna join us?

That stopped Eve for a second. Normally, she would have

jumped at the chance to meet her daughter's friends. But she had made a promise to join Shay for dinner in just a few minutes. As much as she knew she should say yes to her daughter, her heart wanted to join Shay.

She looked up at the reflection staring back at her in the mirror. She'd taken extra time with her makeup. Her hair looked fabulous. Even her dress looked better on her than the last time she wore it. Maybe it was her sun-kissed arms, or the slight pink tint across her nose and cheeks.

She looked and felt alive.

He'd done that to her. And all she wanted was to spend a little more time with him.

Sorry, really tired after my hike today. I'm just going to stay and eat here. Have a great time.

She wasn't lying. She really was tired. Being outside for hours had made her feel good. She missed this. It had been a couple of months since she'd hiked.

While she loved Seattle, it was difficult to get outside in the dead of winter. Less sunlight and constant rain meant she just didn't have the time after she got home from work. Even the weekends since Halloween had been nothing but rain. A wet year, the experts had said.

She needed to change that. She needed to find something she loved to do, outside of work.

Like this. She'd always traveled, told herself she'd do it even more once her daughter was out of the house. Yet here she was, working more than ever.

She sighed, just as her phone buzzed once again.

Okay. I'll probably be home late. We're going clubbing. Don't wait up.

Have fun. Be careful. Don't forget, we have spa appointments at ten.

I won't. See you tomorrow.

This changed things.

She went back into her room and dug her clutch out of her suitcase. She filled it with just the essentials, and tucked her phone inside.

She sat on the edge of the bed and secured her sandals around her ankle. She grabbed her shawl just in case, and headed out the door.

She was a couple of minutes late, but she saw him the moment she walked into the restaurant.

He was sitting at one of the best tables in the place, against a glass backdrop that looked out over the ocean. It was small, but set for three.

He was in jeans with a blazer over a t-shirt. His hair just a little wild.

After checking in with the host, she made her way through the crowded room. He caught sight of her as she approached the table.

Yep, she had his attention. She might have even put a bit more sashay in her swing.

"Hi." He stood. His eyes did that quick up and down thing guys do before settling in closer to her. "Beautiful," he whispered.

"Thanks."

His eyes kept flicking over her shoulder, searching. She left him standing there for just a moment, trying not to laugh.

"She's not here."

She barely got the words out before he planted a kiss on her lips.

"Hi," he repeated.

She gave him another quick kiss before falling into the chair across from him.

"Is she coming later?"

"Nope. She met up with friends. They're going clubbing tonight. So, I guess it's just you and me." She picked the olive out of his martini, popped it into her mouth. "If that's all right."

He grinned.

God, she loved the way his eyes held hers. As if he was studying her, trying to learn all he could.

She shouldn't feel like this, should she?

She was fifty. Almost.

And yet somehow, she felt like she was a college student all over again. Studying abroad and having dinner with a gorgeous man. But this wasn't college, she couldn't act outrageous and jump on a whim. She had a daughter to think about. What kind of role model would she be?

She ordered a glass of wine, and they settled on an appetizer to share.

"You have me at a disadvantage here."

She cocked her head, puzzled. "I do?"

"You said you read about me. You know more about me than I know about you."

"Only what you released in the article. I didn't Google you, Mr Mayfield."

"What if I Googled you?"

That threw her off guard. "You did?"

"No. But I could have," he grinned as he sipped his martini.

"Trust me, it'd be pretty boring. Everything that comes up in my ranking is linked to my job at Shutterbug. You'll find my LinkedIn and Facebook accounts. And that's really about it. I don't post much. I'm more of a lurker than a poster."

"Give me your profile version of who you are. What would Twitter or Instagram tell me?"

"Hmm." She thought about the groups she joined and the things she did online.

"It would tell you I work too much. I have a love affair with vegetarian recipes, though I'm not home enough to cook. I read a lot and have as many books on my nightstand as I do on my Kindle. I love to travel and do it every chance I get."

"Where's the last place you visited?"

"Last spring, a friend and I took a shopping trip to Paris. She found a women-only tour company that offered a one-week trip to discover Paris. We traveled with an American textile designer currently living in the heart of the city."

"That sounds like fun."

"We had a blast. In fact, we had to buy an extra suitcase to bring home all of our deals."

"I love how women have this expert knack of finding *deals*."

"We do, don't we?" She played along with his remark. "The woman that lead the tour was fantastic. She brought us into small boutiques, a perfume shop, home decor spaces, an antique market, a spice shop. We stopped by an artist's workshop and watched her paint these delicate roses onto canvas. It was simply amazing. I had to have one."

"One of your *deals*?" He put his hand in front of his mouth, trying not to laugh.

"Of course. I'll have to show it to you some time."

She sucked in her breath at her words.

That was a very big assumption. To show him meant he'd have to see her place. That meant they continued to build on this relationship, and not treat it as it quite possibly might be:

a holiday tryst.

She held his eyes, contemplating what it would be like to see him again after the New Year. Was it something she'd want? Was it even possible, given where they lived and their busy lives?

He seemed to read her mind. "And that leads back to the question from this afternoon."

She nodded. "Today has taken me by surprise."

"Me too. I didn't come looking for a relationship." He continued, "I also didn't come here to get laid for the weekend."

"Nor did I. This," she motioned between them, "never even entered my mind. I came for my daughter. I came to celebrate Christmas with her, partially because I didn't want to spend it or my birthday alone."

"And I'm happy I got to play a part in your celebration. Honestly, I have no agenda. I think somehow, we managed to show up in each other's space, and I'm happy about that. I've enjoyed being with you. We're both here, same time, same place. We have a lot in common. Do we have to define it any more than that?"

That was something she'd been thinking about since she'd left him in the lobby, returned to her room to shower for the evening.

Why was it she'd been dating, looking for a relationship for years, only to find someone that charged her up in the least likely of places? They had a lot in common, but they didn't live in the same world. Heck, she didn't even know if *he* was dating. She only knew he had loss in his life.

She knew a lot about him losing his mom. But he hadn't said much about his ex. She decided to start there. "I know you said you've recently divorced."

"It was official in May, but it was over long before that."

"What happened?"

"We were married for fifteen years, but the last couple have been challenging. She's a rising lawyer. I've been building and selling a business. We could go days, sometimes weeks without seeing each other."

"I'm sorry." She knew only too well what it was like

living with someone and never seeing them. She'd played that game herself with her ex shortly before they decided to call it quits. "That parts never easy."

"I knew it was over a long time ago. But when I came home early from a business conference at the end of last year and found her in bed with one of the partners from her firm, I filed the next day."

"I'm sorry."

"That's why I wanted to disappear this year. Get as far away from home as I could get. I don't know, maybe I thought flying halfway around the globe would allow me to create new memories. To completely push this last year out of my mind. This place kept coming up on my radar, so here I am."

"How's it working for you so far?" She grinned as she picked up her glass of wine and took a sip.

"It's the best holiday I've had in quite a while."

Damn, he was sexy as hell. His eyes bore deep into her, almost as if he was looking at her on another level. She found it unnerving, in a very good way.

In a way she didn't want to think about, because her daughter was here, somewhere, and the last thing she wanted was to have her walk in on her, him, together.

She chose a safer path. "Why do people do that to each other? Why not call it quits before they hurt each other? Especially by bringing someone into your very own house." She couldn't imagine the pain of finding your spouse with someone else, in your bed. At least her ex had waited until they were divorced.

"Is that what split you and your husband apart?"

"No. Not really. In his words, he decided he wanted to 'spread his wings' and see what else was out there. What he meant was that I was holding him back from 'having fun.' To my knowledge, he never cheated on me. But he sure took up with the ladies once he moved out. And they've been getting younger ever since."

"I've never understood that, for the record. My wife and I chose not to have children for a variety of reasons. And I wouldn't want to start a family now. I'm only forty-six, and I wouldn't mind older kids. Stepkids. But I don't want a family of my own."

"You wouldn't want a little you?"

"No. I'm not quite sure I have the patience for it. Plus, I enjoy my lifestyle too much."

"You travel a lot too?"

"All the time. Or I did. Now, I'm not sure what I'll be doing."

"What do you want to do?"

"I'm still trying to piece it all together. But I have several conferences lined up the first few months of the year. I sit on several boards. And I'm talking to quite a few tech companies about investment opportunities. I've always enjoyed working with startups, and I think turning to angel investing, giving back to young entrepreneurs who need a helping hand, sounds exhilarating. I'm not ready to settle down on any one thing."

"I think now is a good time to be looking around. There's a lot of opportunity out there."

"Have you thought about leaving your job?"

"I find myself in this weird position. My daughter will graduate next year, and outside of maybe living with me while she finds a job, I know for the most part she won't return. I haven't been married in years, but I'm not against another relationship. My dad has a new woman in his life, and they're traveling and living life to the fullest. My brother's happy and doing well with his family. I'm settled. I've been with a company for years, work a job I could do in my sleep. I've thought about doing something else for a long time, but I have no idea what. So, I just keep doing it until I find whatever else I'm looking for."

"That sounds kind of like letting life pass you by."

"I know, it does, doesn't it? And that's the thing. I can sit here and tell you all of this. But I don't know what I want to do. I'm happy. For the most part. Why mess with happiness? I get lots of vacation time, travel a lot. I'm in a good spot."

"Then why do you feel like you want something else?"

"Exactly. That's exactly what I keep asking myself. Over

and over again."

"Maybe you need to do something drastic."

"Like what?"

"Like sail away. Maybe we could buy a sailboat and sail around the Caribbean for a year."

"That sounds awfully tempting."

"It does, doesn't it?"

"And would you be up for that?"

"Maybe." The word slipped out of her mouth. But in her gut, she knew she meant it. "How can I feel so comfortable with you that I would even joke about such a crazy thing?"

He didn't skip a beat. "I have no idea. But I feel it too."

Chapter Nine

"I'm not going to ask you in," Eve lingered outside of her door.

"I don't expect you to."

"Grace said she wouldn't be back until late. Still …"

"Eve, I didn't walk you up here with the hopes of more."

She placed her hands on his chest. "Maybe I want there
to be more. Maybe, just a little."

She kissed him.

It was the kind of kiss like when you've really wanted
chocolate cake, the really decadent kind, but you've been *oh-so-
good* and not had dessert in forever, and then you're at your
favorite restaurant that makes the best chocolate cake in the
entire world, and you order the smallest, low-calorie meal so
you can have the chocolate cake for dessert, and you pop that
first bite into your mouth and almost die …

She seriously thought she was going to die.

Her mind spun like a wheel.

Do it.

Do it.

Just do it already.

You're always so good.

You deserve it.

Live it up.

You're on holiday.

You have separate bedrooms with an entire living-space between you.

You could be quiet.

You could have fun.

Consider it a birthday present to yourself ...

She whimpered as he nibbled on her ear.

She couldn't take it anymore.

She reached down and grabbed his hand. "Come inside."

As she unlocked the door, he took a step back.

"Honestly, Eve, I don't want you to have regrets about this

later."

She turned and faced him, letting the door close once again. "Thank you for that. I have no idea what this is between us or why it happened. I just know I haven't felt like this in a very long time. And maybe it's because it's my birthday, or it's Christmas, or I'm on vacation. Whatever it is, I want this. I do. More than ever. I won't have regrets. You're all I've been thinking of since this afternoon."

One look at his face told her everything she needed to know. He was a good man, she could feel it in her gut. And no matter what happened after they boarded planes and went their separate ways, she wanted him. It was as simple as that.

"And we do have two separate bedrooms." She tipped her head to the left. "I'm on this side, and Grace is on the other. What about you? Are you okay with this?"

He nodded as he snaked an arm around her waist, kissing her forehead. "I am. I've been thinking about you nonstop too. I haven't been with anyone in a very long time. My wife and I … let's just say it was a long time. And I haven't had the energy to look for anything else, not with anyone. There was work. My mom. Life."

"I get it." She kissed his lips. "Do you have anything? A condom?"

He stepped back again, shaking his head. "No. I didn't think. I didn't plan."

She kissed him again. "Lucky for you, my side of the suite came equipped with a goodie basket. And it had three."

He laughed as she raised her eyebrows up and down. "It's definitely my lucky day."

She linked fingers with his, opened up the door, and pulled him inside.

She glanced at Grace's door, which stood open wide. Only darkness coming from inside.

She pulled him towards her room, shut the door, and kicked off her shoes.

She put her hands under his jacket, slipped it off his shoulders, and laid it over a chair.

The moon was high up in the sky, filtering moonlight

across her bed. Glancing out at the night sky, she could see twinkly lights flickering brightly.

"You're beautiful," his hands settled alongside her face. He stopped inches from her face, studying her, before touching her lips. As he came back up for air, he repeated, "So beautiful."

God, she was turned on.

How long had it been?

And why the hell had she waited so long?

She knew why. Because she wouldn't have this feeling with just anyone.

It was him. Everything about him. His look. His attention. Even his smell.

A deep woodsy scent that had her tingling to her core. The one she'd vaguely noticed in the taxi; the same fragrance he'd worn in the van they rode in to the beach. It was her new aphrodisiac.

She pulled his shirt up, placed her hands on his warm chest. Helped push his shirt up and over, sending it sailing onto the floor.

His hands worked just as feverishly, finding the zipper on her dress.

As his fingers trailed downward with the zipper, his hands firmed a grip onto her ass.

She pulled at his belt buckle, unzipping, pushing his jeans down.

She stepped out of her dress, leaving it puddled on the floor.

His breath caught as he took in her lace. She was ever grateful she had a thing for gorgeous lingerie.

She spun, "You like?"

He was on her in an instant.

With hands just under her ass, he lifted her, walked her to the bed. As he lowered her down, she pulled him down with her.

She hadn't done this in, oh, so long. But it was like a bicycle; she knew she never really forgot.

She'd been so used to one man in her life. All her experience came from being with him, giving her ex what he wanted.

And while she knew where to touch, what to do, she quickly found him guiding her hands, telling her what pleasured him.

She returned the favor, sighing when things got good. Saying "yes" and "more" when he did things incredibly right.

And as he slipped on the condom and placed his tip at her core, she felt herself holding her breath, waiting, for the one feeling like no other.

And then …

They sighed together.

And developed their own unique rhythm. Him rocking. Her meeting him, every thrust, every touch.

And just when she got close, he'd pull back.

Again.

And again.

Until she felt she couldn't take anymore.

"Now. Please. Come."

And he spilled everything, while inside her. Falling into

her. Being with her.

After, they lay side by side. Staring, just trying to figure it all out.

"Should I go?" He pushed a strand of hair from her eyes, caressing her cheek.

She moved a leg over his. "No." Then a breath later. "Unless you want to."

"No. I don't." He slow-kissed her once more.

"Why don't we set an alarm for early. I guarantee you Grace won't be getting up early. Plus, I locked my bedroom door."

"You're okay with that?"

She really couldn't believe her luck. He was so thoughtful, caring, concerned with how she felt.

How had his ex ever let him go?

Of course, she knew from experience, that it took two to tango. Time and age often did funny things to perspective.

Right now, they were both here. Enjoying every moment.

She snuggled into him. She turned, picked up her phone, and looked at the time. Three. Dropping the phone back on the end table, she felt his warm body move into her. Spooning her.

"Hi." She felt his hand cup her breast. She trailed her fingers up and down his arm, playing with his hair.

"Hi." He moved just enough; she could feel him on her back, hard, ready.

She wiggled into him, smiling when she heard him groan.

"We only have one more condom left."

She turned over, threw her leg back over him, and pressed against him. "Exactly, we still have one condom left."

He chuckled as his hands started wandering once again.

She reached for the package they'd left on the nightstand. Tore it open, placed it on him, and rolled it down slowly.

Playing as she went, of course.

With him standing at attention, she straddled him,

consumed him.

Then set a rhythm they both enjoyed.

She linked her fingers with his as he shifted closer to the wall. Sitting up, he wrapped his arms around her, pulling her closer. The perfect height for playing with her breasts.

She breathed deeply with every rhythmic move. Her almost meditative state gave her heightened awareness.

She felt it building once again.

What this man did to her, she never expected.

She sat up straighter, looked deep into his eyes, watching, waiting.

She could see it building in him too.

They stared through hooded eyes, feeling every mood.

"I'm … there …" With his hands on her hips, he added energy to their pulse. Deeper. Deeper. Until she felt it too.

"Me … too …"

She wrapped her arms around his neck, hugging him close to her skin. She could feel the tickle of his breath against her neck. As he moved and gyrated inside her.

As their heart rates and breathing returned to normal, they collapsed on the bed one last time, totally wrapped up in one another.

They spoke softly for another hour. Sweet nothings and promises for something more.

And as her phone started humming with a soft tune at precisely five o'clock, he kissed her one more time, rose, grabbed his clothes, and was gone.

Had she dreamed it all? Touching the tender skin on her thigh where he'd left whisker burn, she knew it was real.

She set her alarm for three hours later. She wanted plenty of time to shower before she woke her daughter in the morning. Since they'd be having a spa day together, she thought it to be a good idea to erase any evidence.

And as she drifted off to sleep, she couldn't stop smiling.

Chapter Ten

Eve barged into her daughter's room, reached out, and shook her gently. "Wake up, wake up. We overslept."

"What?" Her daughter sat up, rubbing her eyes.

"Our spa day. Our first appointment is in ten minutes. We have to get downstairs now."

Eve didn't wait for a response. She hustled back to her own room, grabbing a tie for her hair.

"Mom? What do I wear?"

"Just slip on the robe in the closet. Our first appointment is a dual massage out by the pool."

They jogged down the hallway, opting for the stairs instead of waiting for the elevator.

They were greeted and led to a cabana with views of the Mediterranean in the distance. They slipped onto the massage tables and waited for their massages to begin.

The two therapists introduced themselves and began.

Slowly, Eve felt the tension disappear.

She loved massages. Why didn't she do this more? A hint of jasmine was in the air. The waves crashed in the distance. Even though the hotel was at capacity, she couldn't hear anyone from the pool - an added bonus.

It was just her and her daughter. She opened her eyes to Grace's grin from across the cabana. Bliss.

Note to self: do this every holiday from now on.

She closed her eyes, breathed deep, and relaxed. She felt her tightened muscles as the therapist began, and worked to relax as she dug in deep.

She needed more of this.

More massages.

More time away from the office.

More hiking.

More dinners out.

More kissing.

More sex.

Maybe she needed to go sailing.

What would that be like? To hop on a boat and sail away, with no return date in mind?

With a guy she was starting to like?

Her mind drifted as warm hands rubbed her sore muscles.

She needed to clean out the guest room back at her condo. In case she had a guest.

She made a note to fill up a bag with clothes she no longer would wear.

She thought about the email she'd received just yesterday. The one she shouldn't have read before she crawled into bed because she'd promised herself to leave work in the states while she was here in Spain. The one from her boss who told her there was a strong possibility her counterpart from IT may have gotten another job and would be leaving the first of the year. The one that guaranteed she would have a very busy January once she got back to work.

And all of that meant that no matter how much she wanted change in her life, the new year was just going to bring more of the same.

Unless I do something different.

Such as start a company. The way Shay had years before.

Or just quit and play for a year. The way Shay was planning to do.

Or maybe …

"Can I have you lie on your back, please?" The woman peeled the sheet up from her, holding it between them, giving her plenty of privacy to turn.

Eve flipped. The therapist tucked the sheet underneath her arms. She started at her feet, rubbing her heels and her toes.

Eve sank back into her thoughts.

What was stopping her from moving forward? Courage. And a nagging feeling of wondering if she was simply too old to start over with something new.

She'd achieved so damn much in her life. A great home.

A wonderful daughter. A healthy bank account. Vacations whenever she chose. The ability to buy whatever she wanted, whenever she wanted.

What if she tried something new and failed miserably? Then what?

Wasn't that always her biggest holdback?

If she started a business and it didn't work, what would it cost her?

If she trusted someone again with her heart, and he broke it?

Isn't that why she'd been living the way she had for so long?

Eve and Grace followed one of the therapists back inside.

"Your next appointment is in thirty minutes. We have a steam room over here for your use. We have snacks, water, and tea here at the self-serve bar. Lunch will be served after your facials, out near the pool. Can I get you anything?"

"No," they echoed in unison.

Eve made them each a hot tea while Grace placed yogurt, fruit, and granola into two bowls. They ate quickly to have time in the steam room.

Eve slipped off her robe and hung it on a peg, before wrapping a towel around herself and stepping inside. She sat in the corner, leaning back and breathing in the lavender-scented air. She took the tie out of her hair, pulled it back into a tighter bun, and secured it into place.

"What time did you get in last night?" She glanced at her daughter, who was settling in next to her.

"I think it was right before midnight."

"Did you have fun?"

"We did."

"Who's here? Did you know your friends were going to be here?" Eve opened her eyes when her daughter remained silent. "Grace?"

Grace leaned forward, elbows to knees, chin in hands. "I'm sorry, Mom."

Eve moved forward, waiting for an explanation.

"When I told Tanner I was coming to Mallorca, we decided he'd come too. I should have thought more about it. I knew you wanted to spend time with me. And it's your birthday and all. But he's in Spain alone, and I didn't want him to have to be alone for Christmas."

Eve touched her daughter's shoulder. "What are you trying to say? Who's Tanner?"

Grace collapsed back to the wall. "He's my boyfriend."

"Wait. What? You have a boyfriend? Since when?"

"Since Thanksgiving."

"And you didn't tell me?" Eve bit her tongue, trying to keep her frustration at bay.

"I wasn't quite sure what it was."

"When were you planning on telling me this?"

"While you were here?" Grace squeaked out her answer, trying to avoid her mom's stares.

"Is there something wrong with him? Why did you hide him from me?"

Grace stood up, then sat right back down. "Mom, stop. Nothing's *wrong* with him. I just wasn't sure myself."

"And you're sure now?"

She hesitated. A big goofy grin spread across her face. "Yeah, I kinda am."

Eve shook her head. She touched her finger between her eyes. *Ten. Nine. Eight. Seven.*

"Mom, I know I should have said something. Honestly, I'm not sure why I didn't. We met at the Thanksgiving party we had, the one we co-sponsored with the other dorm. I told you about it."

"Yes. I remember that."

"Tanner lives in the other dorm. He's from Maryland. He's a junior at Georgetown. We talked at the party, and we like the same things."

"Okay."

"But we're both busy, so it's not like we even had the opportunity to date. Not exactly. We ended up going to several more dinners together. We're both taking Dr Faulk's course, so we've both been selected to be a part of the consulting week right after the holidays. We just kept running into one another. And, well."

"Well?" She looked at her daughter, waiting for more. "You didn't have to hide him from me."

"I didn't. Not really. He was just more of a friend. And when I Skype with you, we always talk about other things, like school, and trips, and your job. So last week, when it kinda turned into more, I wasn't even sure of what it was. And you were busy getting ready to come here to Spain. How was I supposed to tell you about it? And I didn't even know what to tell you. I'm still not. I mean, I like him and all. But we have a lot of work ahead of us this semester. Then we both have our senior years on opposite ends of the country. And his goal is to stay in DC. And you know I want to travel. I want to work somewhere over here in Europe, at least for a while. How was I supposed to tell you all of that?" Grace finished with tears in her eyes.

Eve wrapped her arm around her daughter into a hug.

"You're rambling."

Grace huffed.

Eve kissed the top of her head. "I get it."

Grace pulled back. "You do? Then could you explain it to me?"

Eve laughed.

Grace's eyes shined, wet with fresh tears. Her cheeks were bright pink from the heat of the steam. She had the scared look she often got when she was a small child. It reminded Eve of all the good times they'd had over the years, and how much she missed having her daughter in her life on a regular basis.

"Tell me about Tanner."

Grace's face lit up. "He's amazing. Yesterday was the first chance we had to spend all day together and not have a class to go to or a paper due. We just walked. We spent three hours at lunch, just talking. We think so much alike. I like his plans for the future. We have so much in common, I am enjoying being with him."

"Why is he here? He decided not to go home for the

holidays?"

"His parents went to California to be with his brother. His brother married last year, and they just had a baby. Originally, Tanner was going home too. Then when this consulting opportunity opened up, he decided to stay."

"You should have mentioned it before. I would happily have included him in our plans."

"I just didn't want you to be upset. You came all this way for me. And I didn't want you to think I wanted to be with him more than you."

"Think about that for a minute. Yesterday you spent the day with him instead of me. If he had joined us, I would have been with both of you."

"Oh. Yeah. Sorry about that."

"No worries. What's done is done. But can he join us for the rest of our time together instead of you running off to be with him?"

"Including tonight for dinner?" Grace grinned.

"I'm thinking you've already invited him."

"Kind of?"

Eve rolled her eyes. "Text him. He's invited. Just have him meet us in the lobby."

"Thanks!" Grace hugged her.

Eve took a deep breath and continued on before she lost her nerve. "And by the way, we'll have a fourth person joining us tonight."

Grace's eyes furrowed. "What? Who?"

"Someone from my tour yesterday. It was only the two of us. And he's here alone for the holidays. I told him he could join us tonight, and he accepted."

"He?"

"Yes," she tried to sound nonchalant. She hoped she was hiding her feelings. "He's from San Francisco. It's kind of a funny story." And she launched into the story of how they met.

"Wow. Sounds like we're quite the pair." Her daughter rose and opened up the steam room door, stepping out. She held it open for Eve to follow.

"What do you mean?"

"Sounds like you've been hiding something from me too."

"What? I just met him."

"Yeah, but I can tell there's something there. I see it in your eyes."

Eve pushed past her, picked up a glass, and filled it with water. It couldn't be that obvious, could it?

"I have no idea what you're talking about. And in any case, I haven't seen you much since I spent time with Shay."

Grace took the glass from her mom and finished the water. "Okay, that's true." She set the glass on a tray reserved for dirty glasses, turned back to her mom, and grabbed her hands.

"I'm excited to meet him. He sounds great. And besides, it's Christmas. The more, the merrier."

A therapist stuck her head inside the room. "Are you two ready for your next appointments?"

They nodded and followed her out the door.

But not before Grace tried to get in the last words. "And

now it looks like we might just have four instead of two for the rest of our activities."

Eve linked arms with her daughter, as they shuffled down the hallway. "I think you're right."

Chapter Eleven

"You look gorgeous!" Grace bounced as she circled her mom. "I love how they did your hair."

They had spent six hours being pampered in every way possible, including hair and makeup. Eve had been a little shocked at the bill, but looking in the mirror, she was glad she'd splurged. It was her fiftieth, after all.

Somehow, Mallorca was turning into a magical place. Something she would never have anticipated a few short weeks ago. Hell, Mallorca hadn't even been on her radar a few short weeks ago.

Eve eyed her daughter, watching as a smile spread across her face while looking at the screen. No doubt, Tanner had texted her something. To think she hadn't even known about him a day ago. Now it was all Grace wanted to talk about.

Which Eve didn't mind. It meant she didn't have to talk more about Shay. So far, Grace assumed he was just someone she'd met on a trip. She knew that would change once they were all together.

Even though Shay promised to keep things platonic at dinner, she wasn't sure she could hold up her end of the bargain. Just thinking about him made her happy. And she knew he'd be feeling pretty *happy* too when he saw her.

Eve knew she looked good. She *felt* good. She felt sexy as hell.

"Are you ready?"

Grace nodded and held the door open to their suite.

Eve placed her key into her bag, grabbed her shawl, and headed out the door.

The elevator opened to the lobby, and they stepped out. Grace was gone in an instant.

Eve stopped and watched as her daughter flung herself into the arms of a very good-looking guy. Her daughter had exceptional taste.

She smiled at the picture the two of them created. Grace had dated some in high school, but nothing serious. She'd had a boyfriend her freshman year of college, but that cooled when they were away for the summer.

She didn't hold back from dating, but she'd never really made it a priority. Grace had her head on her shoulders. She knew what she wanted. Her career mattered, and she wasn't going to let a boyfriend stand in her way.

For that, Eve was grateful.

But that didn't mean she couldn't play a bit. Eve actually encouraged it. She wanted her daughter to experience different relationships. Eve felt it was the best way to grow, to find out who she was before permanently settling down. And only then - hopefully years from now - she could make a good choice for how she lived her life, and who with.

"Hi."

She glanced to her right. Standing next to her was Shay, looking even better than she remembered.

He cleaned up nicely. No jeans tonight. He had on nice

pants, a turtleneck, and a jacket that brought out the color of his

eyes. He smelled good, that spicy, woodsy scent she was

intimately familiar with.

"Did you catch any fish today?"

"I did. And I released every one of them."

"Sounds like a perfect day." She beamed at him.

"Especially for the fish."

She laughed.

She felt his fingers link with her own. Just a gentle

squeeze.

He nodded towards Grace. "Does she know about us?"

"Kind of? She confessed to me today that *he* was the

reason she didn't come along yesterday." Eve nodded towards

the couple. "I didn't even know he existed until this morning.

His name is Tanner. He also stayed here to be part of the

consulting group after the new year. He was going to be alone,

so Grace invited him here. Without telling me. Go figure."

Grace turned to Shay. "I told her how we met and that

we spent the day together yesterday. I told her you were joining us for dinner tonight. But I didn't tell her we made out like college kids last night."

She grinned as she saw a hint of desire cross his face.

"So, she wouldn't do well if I scooped you up and kissed you like she did Tanner just now?"

She glanced back at her daughter, who was clearly enamored with her new boyfriend. But they were separating a little. They were talking, glancing around. Which meant they'd notice the two of them shortly. Better to keep their distance.

"Probably not. I am *Mom*, after all."

He glanced at her sideways, eyes sparkling. "And, Mom's aren't allowed to do those sorts of things?"

"Definitely not." She bit back her laughter.

"Well, if I can't kiss you, I can use my words and tell you how incredibly beautiful you are. You took my breath away when you walked off that elevator. If we were alone, I might tempt you to ignore our reservations for tonight."

Eve suddenly wished her daughter wasn't with them.

She bit back the temptation, especially when she heard

"Mom" coming from across the room.

"I guess that's my cue."

"Lead the way."

Introductions were made. Eve knew immediately she liked Tanner. He was exactly who she would pick for her daughter. Not that she'd ever step in and offer unsolicited advice.

He was well-mannered, looked her in the eye when he spoke, and, more importantly, had nothing but tenderness on his face when he looked at her daughter.

Eve could tell he was smitten with her, even if Grace had downplayed the importance of their relationship.

Together, the four of them sat in the middle of a crowded restaurant, and the hours flew by.

Tanner and Shay hit it off, and spoke at length about the security industry. Tanner had worked at his campus's IT department for the past two years.

Tanner and Grace chatted about their upcoming conference. They'd both spent a great deal of time working on the project, and were equally excited about the connections they'd make during the week.

They shared their favorite Christmases from years past. Eve shared one of her most cherished, when Grace was ten and had made her birthday breakfast in bed. She'd put together plates of cereal, pastries, berries, and a large pot of tea. It had turned out perfectly … until Grace dropped the tray on her, while she was still asleep. It had been a frantic few moments while Eve and her ex woke to a very wet and messy bed. She had everyone rolling with laughter at the description of two adults eyeing each other, and trying to figure out why the bed was wet.

After a second bottle of wine, and the biggest piece of chocolate cake for dessert Eve had ever seen, Grace and Tanner headed out in one direction in search of a nightclub, while Shay and Eve turned the other direction, back towards the hotel.

"That was fun. I've enjoyed meeting your daughter. She has her head on her shoulders. And Tanner seems like a great guy." He wrapped his arm around her shoulders, pulling her in close.

Even though she'd brought a shawl with her, the temperatures had dropped enough, it was a chilly walk. Plus, who was she to argue with a chance to get closer to Shay.

"I like him too. He's a good fit for Grace. And was it just me, or did he seem like he was head over heels for her?"

He chuckled. "That's one way of putting it. I think he's definitely enchanted with her."

"This should be interesting. Grace has such strong convictions for what she wants to do, who she wants to become. She's not willing to let anything, or anyone, stand in her way. It's not like when I was young."

"How old were you when you married?"

"A year out of college. We met our senior year. We graduated and got engaged all in the same month."

"I was quite a bit older. I was twenty-nine."

"That's because you're a guy. Nobody ever questioned guys back then. Even though the world told us we could do anything as women, there was still this underlying expectation in college that it was our time to find *the one*."

"How did I not know this?"

"Because you're a guy," she grinned. "I'm hopeful because that expectation seems to have left this generation behind."

"I would agree. I work with a lot with the people. Marriage is the furthest thing from their minds. Which, looking back, isn't necessarily a bad thing."

"Would you ever marry again?"

They stopped on a street corner, where a group of carolers in nineteenth-century costumes went by. A group of fun-loving vacationers followed close behind, singing at the top of their lungs.

Shay turned, facing Eve. She watched as his eyebrows scrunched together, in deep thought.

"I don't think so. I'm not against commitment. And I'd love to fall in love again, this time with the right person. But I'm not convinced I would ever need a wedding band or a certificate to formalize it."

"I agree."

Eve had thought about it a lot.

She wanted love again. She'd dated here and there.

But marriage, it had been out of her vocabulary for so long. And after raising a daughter and experiencing the world, she wasn't sure if she wanted to travel that road again.

She was enjoying her life, loving her freedom. She was happy, healthy, and financially independent.

Finding someone who was her equal excited her.

Someone who inspired her, loved her, and wanted to see the world with her, she'd put that on her bucket list a couple of years before.

But marriage didn't give any of that. In fact, it complicated it. At least in her opinion.

Maybe she'd found a man who thought the same thing?

The streets were decked out in reds and greens. Sparkly lights lit up the front of every restaurant and store. Windows were filled with magical surprises, drawing people in. Families were milling about, arms packed with brightly colored packages as they finished their holiday shopping.

"You know, I used to marvel as a young girl at all the pretty lights everywhere this time of year. I was convinced they put them up, just for me. It always made my birthdays so special."

"How's this one going for you?" He leaned down and touched his lips to hers.

She closed her eyes and felt herself fall into his kiss.

Music was all around them. She heard jingle bells on a carriage that was passing by. Church bells off in the distance. And the constant chatter and laughter as people milled around talking and sharing.

"Pretty good," she whispered as her eyes fluttered open, catching his gaze.

"Pretty good? What would it take to push it to excellent?"

More kisses.

And a whole lot of heat.

How could she have been chilled just a few minutes earlier?

She could easily melt into this guy. He was doing everything right.

And if he kept kissing her this way, she might want even more. She might just drag him up to her room again. *Happy birthday to me!*

"I want …" she managed to whisper in between kisses.

" Me too …" Another kiss.

"And look," he pulled three condoms from his pocket, palming then into her hand. "I had a basket too."

She roared with laughter. "Then I guess we better get back to the hotel."

Chapter Twelve

Eve woke to the sound of chimes. She could hear her phone making the familiar sound off in the distance. She rose, and followed the noise.

She grinned as she saw over a dozen texts waiting for her, each wishing her a happy fiftieth birthday.

She sent back responses, thanking each person before dropping her phone on the bed.

After a quick shower, she was ready for the day.

She'd treated herself to a new dress before she left home, a perfect choice for her birthday. She smiled at her reflection in the mirror as she turned, the soft fabric swishing around her legs.

A touch of lipstick, the necklace from her daughter, and she was out of her room and knocking on her daughter's bedroom door.

"Happy birthday, Mom!" Grace squealed as she opened the door. She wrapped her arms around Eve's neck, giving her a familiar squeeze.

One more reminder of how much Eve missed mornings with her daughter.

But she was here now, and Eve planned on taking every advantage of the next two days, before an early morning flight flew Grace away, back to the mainland. Back to reality.

Arm in arm, they left their suite, and headed down to the restaurant for a quick breakfast.

Eve had thought a lot about how she wanted to spend her fiftieth birthday. She'd been planning it since her forty-ninth. Her ideas had included different trips, different activities. She'd even settled on a bakery for a cake.

But now, she was grateful all her planning had changed just two weeks before. This was far better than any of her ideas. She sat watching her daughter and two men she was beginning to think the world of. As they all interacted over pastries and coffee, she realized she was glad her original ideas hadn't worked out.

At precisely ten, they headed to the lobby to meet their tour guide for the day. Touring wineries would be perfect for her birthday festivities.

Shay had spoken with the tour guide the night before, telling him it was her birthday. The guide had balloons and streamers inside the van, and had the entire group sing happy birthday.

All three vineyards had been ready and waiting to make her day extra special. She even had a small cake waiting for her at the last place they visited.

And the photographs. Her daughter made sure she covered every angle. Between the images Grace forwarded her and the selfies she captured herself, there wasn't a moment uncovered.

After a day of surprises and wine tours, they reached the hotel just in time to make their dinner reservations. Grace ran their purchases back up to their room before they all took their seats.

Christmas Eve was the one time of year the restaurant changed the way they served. Instead of menus, the chef had prepared a seven-course meal. The salad followed the appetizer, with the main entree being a showstopper. Eve pulled her phone out once more, to capture every dish for posterity.

The restaurant was packed with other visitors who had no intention of turning in early. All were waiting for the town's main attraction, a Christmas tradition at the town cathedral just before midnight. Lights, song, and festive caroling would occur throughout the streets as people from all over rang in one of the most memorable nights of the year.

Eve could hardly wait.

Somewhere between dessert and coffee, Shay pulled her up for dancing to the beat of the small band that played in the lobby. She grabbed his hand, laughed as he twirled her around and around.

And just as they slipped into their chairs, the promise of a sweet treat being placed on the table, Shay dropped a small box at her place setting. A bright red box with silver ribbon sparkled in anticipation.

She faced him for a moment, a question in her eyes. "What's this? You didn't have to get me anything."

"I know I didn't. But I'm having so much fun this holiday, and when I passed by this yesterday, it called out your name. Just a little something to remember your fiftieth by." He grinned, picked up the box, and held it out to her.

She slipped off the ribbon, carefully undid the paper. Took the lid off the box, and held her breath peering inside.

A silver bracelet with two gleaming pearls laid inside.

He picked it up, unhinged the clasp, fastened it on her arm.

"Shay, it's beautiful."

"Remember when we were window-shopping last night? I saw you eyeing the pearls. I slipped over early this morning, and this one captured my attention. The salesperson said these are Majorica pearls. I thought it was fitting to help you remember this vacation."

He twisted it so the pearls sat on top. His fingers lingered, rubbing the pearls. "Now you own two."

Eve shivered at his touch.

She took a deep breath, held it, then slowly let it go. She did it again, checked her emotions, then looked over at her daughter.

Eve bit back a smile as she watched her daughter giving her a little thumbs up.

Grace had been encouraging her to date since she left for college. It was clear in Grace's eyes she approved.

Eve held her wrist out for her daughter to see. She touched the delicate piece, awed by the way it gleamed in the light.

She snuck glances at Shay, who was clearly pleased with his purchase.

Where had he come from? How had this happened?

Somewhere deep inside, she felt a tug of woefulness, suddenly dreading the plane ride home.

Back to Seattle, back to work, back to life.

All she could think about was: she didn't want to go home. She didn't want her old life.

She felt like a different person.

Had it really been less than a week?

She'd changed. She'd been seeking it for so long, she was overwhelmed at how fast it had come.

Was this the sign she needed? Was this her push to move forward?

Would this be the start of her second act?

The wait staff dropped off one final glass of champagne, which Grace used to toast her mother.

A little before midnight, the two couples followed the crowd to the city center to participate in the festivities. They sang until their voices were hoarse.

Then in the wee hours of the morning, they each retired to their rooms, with the promise of brunch together late in the morning.

Eve was too excited to go to sleep. She relived every

moment, pulling out her phone several times and going through the pictures. Touching her necklace from her daughter, and the bracelet from Shay.

Where had he come from? Why now? Why here?

It's not she hadn't been looking for someone these past few years. But every date, every choice had been wrong. Yet when she least expected, she'd found someone whose values were the closest to hers, whose dreams and hopes reflected hers.

She knew it from his very first glance. It was the way he looked at her, cared for her.

The way he laughed, paid attention to her, and gave her his undivided attention. Like he truly wanted to hear what she had to say.

Something she hadn't found in the guys she'd dated.

She loved her life, right now. She was happy being her age. And she was looking forward to moving through her fifties. She truly felt like she was on top of the world.

She loved being here in Mallorca with her daughter, and now, two new special friends. She loved exploring, looking forward to each day, instead of living in a world that was quickly becoming boring.

This was something she could get used to.

In fact, maybe it was time she did.

The thought of going back to an office suddenly made her nauseous.

Maybe it was time for her to move on.

If she could only figure out to what. She was too young to sit at home day after day. Maybe she could take a few lessons from Shay.

He'd captured her attention with his talks of angel investing. And though she had no idea of how she'd implement, it was something she had the funding for. And it could be exciting, especially if she could help fund women-owned businesses.

Just think of all she could learn!

How had she been so complacent for so long?

She knew the answer revolved around her daughter. She'd been busy raising her, and getting her the best schooling.

But now that she was living life on her own, maybe it was time for her to move on.

She glanced at the clock.

She put down her phone, and turned off the light.

Tomorrow was another day. And if she didn't get a good night's sleep, she'd never be up in time for brunch.

Chapter Thirteen

"Bye, baby," Eve wrapped her arms around her daughter, hugging her close. "I'm going to miss you so much."

"I'll miss you too, Mom."

Grace promised to text as soon as she got back to her dorm.

Eve hugged Tanner, feeling like he was now a close friend, someone she was sure she'd see again. She'd seen it in her daughter's eyes.

She got back the hotel just in time to see Shay rolling his luggage off the elevator. She met him halfway across the hotel with a hug and a kiss.

"Hi," she breathed him in as she wrapped her arms around him. She glanced up at his face, wishing she had a few more days with him.

He kissed her lips. Lingered, nibbling at the corners.

"Wanna have lunch before I head to the airport?"

"Yes." She kissed him hard.

"Good." He kissed her back. He linked his arm around her waist, grabbed his suitcase, and found a place to sit in the restaurant.

The time seemed to zip by. They talked about everything and nothing.

And while she was making small talk about the weather, how long of a flight it was back to the west coast, and what they each hoped the new year would bring, she found herself dreading the moment of letting him go.

She wasn't that kind of woman. She didn't get hung up on a guy.

Sure, she wanted to date more. But it was more for companionship, having someone close to talk with, and, of course, the sex.

Being here with Shay had opened up her eyes to that

possibility in a way she'd never found with the other guys she dated. It made her realize how alone she was going to be when she returned home. And dammit, she was lonely.

She was dreading going back to her old life.

It just wasn't fun anymore. It felt like drudgery instead of excitement.

She knew she was ready for something more, but she hadn't realized just how much.

When they finally paid the bill, she linked her fingers with his as they strolled to the lobby. He stopped at the front desk to tell them he was ready to leave.

He turned towards her, placed his hand on her cheek, touching his lips gently to hers. "Thanks for the incredible holiday."

"Thanks for sharing it with us."

"I'm so glad we met. I'll give you a call next week. We'll find a date that works for both of us."

"Okay." She bit back the tears, wondering if they would indeed find the time. Or if this entire experience would just fade away.

What was she doing? This wasn't her.

How many times had she preached to her daughter, don't get hung up on a guy.

And here she was, *getting hung up on a guy!*

But as she looked deep into his eyes, she just didn't care.

This weekend had made her feel so good, so alive. It also made her realize all she'd been missing.

No more.

Her eyes were open. And no matter what happened after today, she wasn't going to close them.

She wanted to live fully, to experience life. Not just doing things she'd done for half her adult life.

She had some serious thinking to do.

But for now, she had to say goodbye.

"I wish you could stay," she kissed him gently.

"Me too. But I've had this meeting scheduled for weeks. I have to be there."

"I know."

"I'm sure I can get to Seattle in the next couple of weeks. And maybe you can come down to the Bay Area too. Or maybe we can plan another trip somewhere warm."

"Like Hawaii? I love Hawaii in February."

"Perfect."

They heard the driver call Shay's name. He gave her one final kiss.

And then he was gone.

Eve sat in the restaurant, pen in hand, creating her resolution list. The new year was just around the corner, and she was going to make it a very good year.

Be fluent in Spanish. She'd had it on her list for the last three years. She'd been so good at it back when she was in college. This trip had reminded her how easily it could come back if she put in the work. She was surprised at how easily she'd understood the language.

Travel more. Yep, that was important too. She should be

able to complete that goal, since her daughter was determined to live overseas. She had to visit her once in a while.

And then there was Hawaii too.

She grinned, chewing on the end of her pen.

He had said yes to a trip to the islands before he left. Would it really happen?

She caught her breath, thinking about all the possibilities.

The two of them on the beach. They two of them in the pool. The two of them sharing a bed …

She jumped when her phone vibrated on the table.

Seeing it was her daughter, she touched the screen.

"Hi."

"Hi, Mom, we made it back."

"How was the flight?"

"Good. Crowded. It's pretty quiet here."

"That's good. Maybe you can get a lot done for your conference next week."

"I hope so. Tanner's coming over in a bit. We're going

to work on our projects and have dinner. Then we meet with the whole group tomorrow bright and early."

Eve chuckled. She knew in her daughter's mind, bright and early meant before ten. Old habits die hard.

"Well, you two have fun. And keep me up to date on what's happening. I can't wait to hear all about next week."

"I'll talk with you when I can."

"No problem. I love you, baby."

"I love you too, Mom." And she was gone.

In a lot of ways, she envied her daughter. She'd love to be that excited about something in her future.

Instead of dreading the day she had to go back to work. To more reports and training sessions. To more overtime that she didn't really care about.

She looked down at her resolution list again.

Self-care. She needed a to-do item about self-care. She'd been reading a book on the plane over that stated career women were the worst at having outside interests. She knew she needed to find something to fill her hours, to give her a chance to say "no" more often to overtime.

Her Pilates class wasn't enough. She needed more. Like a painting class, the book had suggested. Or maybe writing a book.

The book had stated almost nine in ten had "write a book" on their bucket lists. Did she? Could she do it? She wouldn't even know where to start.

So she stuck with something simpler. She listed "sign up for a class" as her goal. She'd login a little later and see if she could find something new in her community.

The waiter stopped by, offering her another pot of hot water for her tea. She nodded, selected another tea bag, and filled her cup to the brim.

She watched as a group of six sat down at the table next to hers. Six women with American accents, all laughing and talking at once. They had backpacks and water bottles, floppy hats on top of their heads. They looked wind-blown and happy, with rosy cheeks and happy smiles.

She couldn't help but listen as they talked about their

morning. A sailing expedition to take in the sites of Mallorca from a different vantage point.

They ordered margaritas, and seemed to settle in.

Eve couldn't stop grinning. They looked like they were having so much fun together. She started wondering how they knew each other.

Maybe sorority sisters from long before. She could tell they were all about her age.

Or maybe they were childhood friends, catching up on a year-end vacation.

She listened as they spoke about their day. And about their plans over the next few days.

The more she listened, the more she could tell they were with a travel group. And clearly, the one on the end facing her was the leader.

She was intrigued.

She finally stood and walked over to the table. "I couldn't help but notice how much fun you're all having. Are you with a group?"

The leader shook her hand. "Hi, I'm Niki Burns. I run a company called Single Women Travel. I organize groups just like this one throughout the year. We travel together to stay safer and have more fun as single ladies. This group here is a few of my best customers. They've all been on several trips over the past two years. And since none of us had prior commitments over the holidays, we decided to spend ten days together."

Now Eve was intrigued. "What an interesting concept. You do this regularly?"

"Yep. I have thirty trips on the books for next year, and we'll be booking even more for next fall."

"Wow." Eve's mind was racing.

She'd added "travel more" to her resolution list just a few minutes before. But she'd assumed she'd travel with her daughter, her father, or maybe even with someone like Shay.

She hadn't considered booking a trip with a tour group, especially with a small group of women. "I didn't even know that was possible," she whispered, more to herself than to anyone.

Niki laughed. "You'd be surprised at how many women add traveling to their bucket list, but are too nervous to do anything about it. I make it easy."

"What a great business."

"Thank you. I worked for Expedia for twenty years. I traveled all the time. A few years before I quit, I started traveling with groups similar to mine. Eventually, I decided I could do it better. This will be my third year in business."

"Congratulations. Where are you located, Niki?"

"Seattle."

"I knew it when you said Expedia. I work with Shutterbug."

"I love that company. I've used a bunch of your stock images for my website."

"Could I possibly have your business card? Or even just your website? I'd love to check out your offerings."

"I'll do you even better. If you have a few minutes, why don't you pull up a chair? We're all enjoying a late lunch, and then a few hours to ourselves, before we take in a play later tonight. I'd be happy to chat with you further."

"Okay. I don't mind if I do."

Chapter Fourteen

Three hours later, Eve finally sat back in her chair, losing herself in her thoughts. She'd been chatting with Niki for hours, and her mind was whirling.

After the ladies in Niki's group had said goodbye, the two continued to chat.

Eve started by asking her about Niki's travel destinations. But quickly, it turned into a business discussion.

And just as quickly, the two became fast friends. They discovered their lives had intertwined multiple times living in the Seattle area. They lived with only five miles between them. Both divorcing while their kids were in high school. And now, focusing on their second acts, trying to figure out what to do with the life ahead of them.

"How many employees do you have?"

"Seven, including me. Katie is tech. She runs my website and keeps up with ad design. Then I have Peggy, who I can best describe as an office manager. She kind of does everything and anything. I don't know how I'd survive without her. "

"I have an assistant at Shutterbug just like her."

"Then there's Joyce, who does all of my marketing. And I've hired two additional travel leaders to help me with my tours."

"And you've done all of this in two years?"

"Uh-huh."

"Wow, I'm impressed."

"I doubled my business in the second year. I want to do it again this coming year. I think that I can."

"Totally. I know a lot of women who I think would be excited about this."

"Exactly. So, Eve," Niki paused for effect, took a sip of water, and leaned in closer to the table. "Have you ever considered leaving Shutterbug?"

Eve felt a little zing travel through her body.

Had she ever considered leaving her current position? Only a million times. She just had never figured out what for.

She loved being a part of the team in the early years, when she did a little bit of everything. She loved being in on the ground floor, and adding to the bottom line of the company.

And the people. Some of her very best friendships had been built from within.

Now, they were all moving off in their own directions. Which is why Eve had been itching for the past year to make changes of her own.

"I have, actually. Ever since my daughter went off to college, I've been trying to figure out what's next. And since I haven't put my finger on it yet, I'm still doing what I've done in the past."

"Would you consider a position with my company? Would you be interested in talking further once we get home?"

Eve nodded. "Possibly. Maybe. Yes! I love what you've told me. And the concept seems very rewarding. Plus, I've been looking for ways to bring more travel into my life. This might just be the way to do it."

"I don't have a position I'm hiring for at the moment. I'm just always on the lookout for people who I think would be a good fit for the team. And I like your story; I think you could help us grow to the next level."

"Do you have any idea for how big you're thinking of growing?"

Niki chuckled, "I think I'd like to copy one of my mentors, Rick Steves."

Eve laughed. "Nothing like thinking big. He built an empire over the past couple of decades."

"I know. And he's in our own backyard. I met him once."

"Really?"

"Yep. We were doing a travel expo last summer in Seattle, and I sat by him at a dinner. I've used some of his ideas to grow this past year."

"I know you're leading this group this week. Do you

handle a lot of the tours?"

Niki grinned. "Obviously, that's where I started. I did them all. But I've added so many this past year, and I couldn't do it without my staff. I'm trying not to do more than one a month. Any more just doesn't give me the time I want to work on my business."

"Is that why you want office help?"

Niki nodded. "I've been on the lookout for someone who can help me grow my systems. Hiring travel guides is the easy part; people love getting paid to travel. I already set up my own system early with how I want the tours to function. So, it's the business growth I want to focus on this year. And after talking with you today, I think you might be a good addition. We'll have to talk more, of course, But I am excited about this. I'm a pretty good judge of character, and I think we've hit on something big."

Eve nodded. "I think so too. I've been on the lookout for something other than Shutterbug for a while now, but I've never found something that captured my interest. You're the first person I've spoken with who's done that for me."

Niki grabbed her phone, touched the screen, and tapped. "We get back the night of the second. What does that week look like for you?"

Eve did the same with her mobile. "Other than work, I don't have a lot going on."

"We could meet for dinner."

"Thursday works for me."

"Perfect! I'll connect with you later, and we can firm up the details. Can you send me your contact info?"

Eve added Niki's number to her contact list, and sent her the info in a text.

"I better get going. The ladies and I are heading out for dinner in just a bit."

"I'm sorry I kept you so long." Eve jumped up, pushed her chair in, and gathered up her stuff.

"Not at all, this was perfect. More than good. This has given me a burst of energy for the new year. Thank you for that. I'm so glad we met."

"My pleasure. I'll be looking forward to our meeting next month."

They chatted as they strolled to the elevators and gave a quick hug as the doors open to the second floor. "Happy New Year," Niki said as she walked out, with the doors closing behind her.

Eve leaned against the back wall while she rode to her floor.

Fate. It was the only word that kept flashing through her brain. Fate had her decide to spend the afternoon in the restaurant, planning her future. She'd canceled a tour she'd booked earlier, thinking she'd do it herself. But as the time approached, the only thing calling her name was a chance to sit down and relax and think about her future.

It was fate that led to a wonderful group of women to sit down next to her. Fate had her open up a conversation, one that might just change her life for good.

Her flight was leaving in the morning for Barcelona. She was spending two nights there, just enough to take in a couple of museums. And then she'd be off to the airport. Back home to Seattle, and a chance at changing her life forever.

Her open suitcase lay on the floor. She put a few more items into it, then selected a pair of jeans for dinner. She pulled on a t-shirt and buttoned her favorite blazer into place. Her comfortable slip-on shoes completed the look.

Then she went out one last time to walk around town, looking into shop windows, stopping for small plates of food, and snapping photos of everything that caught her eye.

Three days later, she pulled her luggage behind her as she stepped off the elevator, walking towards her own flat.

She was home at last. Back to darkness and rain, just past four in the afternoon. With a couple of days left of vacation, she decided to order in and save filling her refrigerator up for the next morning.

With an order of Chinese food on a plate, and a glass of wine by her side, she flipped the television on for the first time in two weeks.

And, there he was.

Shay.

Being interviewed for a business show, on his investment strategies for new start-ups.

She'd only heard from him twice; once when he landed, and once wishing her a great flight home.

In truth, she hadn't expected more.

She knew both of their lives were just too busy to make whatever this was between them work.

She may have dreamed about it once or twice. She would have loved to take things further.

But it was what it was. It would always bring back fond memories. She touched her bracelet that encircled her wrist. She hadn't removed it since he clasped it into place.

She turned up the sound and listened to his voice.

The interviewer had just asked him a question. Shay stopped and pondered before giving him his response.

"If you're going to start up something new, you have to

commit fully out. You must be willing to do anything and everything to give it its best shot. Because no matter what your goals are, no matter what opportunity you're presented with, the only way to be successful at it is if you dig in and put in the work."

"That sounds like good advice for everything in life," the interviewer chuckled. "My daughter started college this year, and I told her something similar when I dropped her off."

Shay nodded. "Exactly. I think it works for just about everything. It's the only way you can truly change your life."

As a commercial started rolling across the screen, Eve hit mute. Shay's advice touched her about everything in her life.

She'd been thinking about Niki and possibly switching companies since she'd met her. And the more she thought about it, the more excited she became.

She still wanted to run the numbers, see what Niki had to offer.

But she didn't need to take a job for the paycheck. Right now, she wanted to do something to learn and grow.

171

And if everything went right, as she very well expected, she'd be putting her notice in soon, and going to work in a new industry.

And it thrilled her to the bone.

Shay's face popped back up onto the screen. She felt a familiar tug deep inside.

Damn, he was good looking. And his voice. It did something to her.

Could she find a way to see him again? Should she be the one to try and connect?

She yawned, realizing just how tired she was.

She bit her lip, thinking about creating a life she could love once again.

Travel and a new job were only two of the things she wanted right now.

The other was a companion.

And while it may or may not be Shay, she promised herself she'd connect with him again soon.

Maybe even as soon as tomorrow.

Chapter Fifteen

Eve swirled what was left of her tea in her mug. It was tepid at best. Still, she didn't have the energy to rise from her chair and walk into the kitchen for a refill.

This was normally her favorite spot in her home. The wall of glass looked out to the city below. Her sofa was positioned perfectly to take in the view.

But today, it was just another rainy, cold day, even if it was the last day of the year.

She'd agreed to meet her friends at a local restaurant, before heading out to a party in celebration. Sitting here, she didn't feel like partying. She didn't feel like much of anything.

She was excited about the New Year. She'd spent hours writing pages in her journal, contemplating quitting her job and starting something new.

But now, on December thirty-first, the only thing she wanted was a date.

She'd called Shay not once, but twice since returning home. She'd left messages both times, and had yet to hear back.

He's busy, she told herself.

He'll call when he's ready.

How come now that she'd made up her mind to pursue whatever had started between them, he wasn't responding?

Maybe he has a date for tonight. Maybe he's found someone else.

Then she chastised herself for this line of thinking. She was much too old to get wrapped up in a guy. She didn't do this. *She wouldn't get hung up on a guy!*

She wouldn't. She was her own person. She easily did things on her own.

And she was going to do just that tonight.

Her mind was settled. That was that. She dropped her mug into the sink and was about to head to her room for a shower when her doorbell rang. She picked up her phone, tapped, and looked at the video feed to see who it was.

There, standing at the door, was a large bouquet of flowers, held by a man she didn't recognize. The arrangement was beautiful, filled with reds, purples, and yellows together in a colorful vase.

"Hello?"

"I have a delivery for Eve Nichols."

"That's me. I'll be right down."

She shoved her feet in her shoes at the door before taking the elevator down.

"Hi, I'm Eve."

"Then these are for you."

"Thank you. They're beautiful!"

"You're welcome. And have a Happy New Year."

"You too." She tipped him generously, then held onto the vase as she rode back up. She placed them on the counter, and searched for a card as her doorbell rang once more.

"Hello?" She glanced at the video feed and saw another

man standing there with a big package tied up with a bow.

"I have a delivery for Eve Nichols."

This was getting ridiculous. But she couldn't help but smile.

"I'll be right there."

She grabbed the card she'd pulled from the flowers, and shuffled back into her shoes, back to the elevator. She opened up the envelope, and read it on the way down.

Just because ...

She caught her breath. It didn't say who it was from. It didn't have to. She knew.

The doors opened to a smiling man who held a big box wrapped in black, with a large gold ribbon tied up in a bow.

"Thank you," she said as she gave him a tip, and again went searching for a card. *Nothing.*

She maneuvered upstairs, to her dining room table, dropped the box, untied the ribbon, and lifted off the top. There

176

amongst layers of tissue paper was black lace. As she lifted it from within, she recognized it.

She'd admired it in a shop window, back in Mallorca. On the night she'd spent walking with Shay, admiring pretty things in the windows.

That could only mean one thing …

Holding the dress close, she rifled through the tissue paper, looking for a card. At the bottom, she found a note.

Because you'll look great in it.

She was walking back to her bedroom when the doorbell chimed again. She tapped the icon on her phone and saw a third person waiting with a small package in hand. He had on a baseball hat, so that she couldn't see his face.

"Hello?"

"Delivery for Eve Nichols."

She grinned. "Just a minute."

She laid the dress gently on her bed. Then repeated her

actions, back down to the lobby.

The elevator doors opened, and she stepped out. Right into the arms of Shay.

She squealed, "You're here!" She linked her fingers as they reached around his waist.

"Yep."

"How? Why? You never returned my calls."

"Sorry about that. My week has been crazy. And by the time I thought of calling, I figured this would be better."

"But how? The dress?"

"Remember when you and Grace just had to visit the lingerie shop, and Tanner and I did our own thing? I went back to that little shop we'd found the night before and bought it. I knew I could surprise you somehow," he kissed her hard.

Here he was, standing before her. She felt her heart swell with anticipation.

His eyes, twinkling as bright as ever.

His hair, a little longer and curlier than on the island. She wrapped a curl around her finger, remembering how it looked in the early morning light.

And his face, god, his face. Warm. Handsome. Filled with adoration.

She touched his lips with her fingertips. He gently nibbled.

"So, we're you? Surprised?" he asked.

She jumped and wrapped her legs around his waist as the elevator doors opened. He strode in, walking her back into the wall for support. "Very."

Eve linked her fingers with his, pulling him into her condo. She gave him a quick tour, let him take in the view, before leading him down the hall.

"And here's my bedroom," she turned, facing him, linking her other hand with his. Pulled him just inside the threshold.

"I can't believe you're here."

"I can't believe I haven't seen you in a week."

"How long are you here for?"

"I don't have a ticket back. I'm kind of winging it. I have a couple of meetings set up this here this week, so I figured I'd take it one day at a time."

"Okay."

"Are you okay I'm here?"

She didn't tell him with words. Instead, she showed him with action.

Instead of moving towards him, she stepped back. Pulled her sweatshirt over her head. Again, thankful she always wore her best undies.

"I was about to take a shower, and get ready for a party tonight." She threw her shirt, so it landed near his feet. Then took another step backward, towards her bathroom.

He kicked off his shoes, taking a step towards her. "I like parties."

"I didn't say you were invited," teasing, she bit her lip, looking at him through hooded eyes.

God, he was so incredibly good looking. And she was horny as hell.

She was ready to tease, and by the look on his face, she knew he was feeling it too.

She shimmied out of her yoga pants, kicking them off to the side. She turned, giving him a view he seemed to like.

His shirt flew off one direction, his jeans in the other. And with a skip and a jump, he was on her. Hugging her. Kissing her. Like there was no tomorrow.

They ran out of hot water, long before they were satiated with each other.

Three minutes to midnight, Shay picked up a glass of champagne and held it out to Eve. He took one more from the tray, and held it up to hers.

The festivities were in full swing all around them.

After dinner with friends, they'd followed them all to a party at a local hotel.

Balloons were swaying to the beat just above them, tied in a net, waiting to spill at the stroke of midnight.

The band was finishing one last tune, before the

countdown to New Year's began.

She kissed him hard as they melded together, swaying to the beat of the song.

"Hey, no kissing. Not before midnight."

Her best friend bumped her with her hip. Eve grinned, then looked back up at Shay. "They all like you."

"I like them too."

"Not as much as I like you, though."

"You like me?"

"Mmm-hmmm."

He couldn't keep his hands off her.

Nobody noticed. Everyone around them was playing, singing, clinking glasses, and having a good time.

"Think I could spend the night tonight? I forgot to get a reservation."

She tipped her head, pretended to think for a moment, before telling him, "Yes."

And at the stroke of midnight, standing there with all her friends, and a man she was starting to care a lot about, she rang in the New Year.

Excited about the future.

Possibly a new career.

Maybe a new relationship.

At fifty, she was more than ready.

Second act, here I come!

Want To Read A Book For FREE?

Marketing whiz Ann Mathison is tired of her monotonous life. With a job she could do in her sleep, and a life that is anything but exciting, she takes a trip to paradise with her two best friends to relax and recharge.

But what happens when a big idea sparks her interest and has her dreaming of starting her own business? Will Liz Cohen and Kate Hendricks agree to join her?

Looking for new careers, new lives, success … and maybe even a little romance … brings the three friends back together in one city, working on a project that just may change their lives forever.

Watch out midlife, here we come!

LoriOsterberg.com/start-reading-for-free

About The Author

After running several successful businesses, Lori Osterberg decided it was time to reinvent herself once again. Facing an empty nest and too much normal suburbia lifestyle in front of her, she talked her husband into selling off their 3300 square foot home, sell two-thirds of their stuff, all for the chance to slow travel the world. When not traveling, she finds a friend or two to share a good bottle of wine, visits tea factories, dances the night away at outdoor concerts, eats her way through farmers markets, and day-dreams about the next set of characters she lives vicariously through. She's currently writing books and living the dream in the Pacific Northwest.

You can learn more at:

https://LoriOsterberg.com

Lori on Instagram: @LoriOsterberg

Lori on Facebook: facebook.com/LoriOsterbergAuthor

Please turn the page for an exciting sneak peek of

Lori Osterberg's

The Creative Standalone Series

The Writer

1

Chapter One

She needed this workout. Bad.

He had her so mixed up. And so full of energy. She had no idea what to do with all of this pent up frustration.

Yeah, she was going with that. Frustration. She snorted knowing full well it wasn't just frustration.

She slid on her favorite workout shorts. Pulled the tank over her head and moved it into place. With a quick tie of her shoes, she was ready to go.

It was late; she was the only one in the gym. Tonight, intensity was her middle name.

One mile on the treadmill.

One hundred pull-ups.

One hundred pushups.

One hundred bodyweight squats.

Back to the treadmill for another mile.

She moved to the weights. And as she adjusted the bar-bell, she caught her breath. She knew he was there. Could feel him there.

She looked up, into the mirror, searching. Caught just a glimpse, in the corner, watching.

So he wanted to play that game?

She picked up the barbell, started in with the repetitions. Up. Down. Flexing. Moving.

She knew she looked good, standing there just a little sweaty, breathing hard.

Up. Down. Up. Down.

As she counted down ... seven, six, five, four ... she saw him move in.

He stepped to her side, searching for her eyes in the mirror.

He took her breath away. But she wasn't going to let him see how he impacted her. How bad she wanted him.

Three. Two. One.

She put the barbell back into place. And as she stood up,

he was there. Behind her.

He wrapped an arm around her, pulled her in. He breathed deeply. "You're so fucking hot." He nibbled her neck, behind her ear, right where she liked it. Trailed his tongue down her spine.

She arched into him, moaned. How did he do that? How did he turn her into a quivering mess? How had she survived without him?

She pressed against him, feeling every last hard inch of him. Her hand traced down his abs, down his rock-hard stomach. More. She wanted, oh, so much more ...

"Dammit." Kelly jumped as her phone rang next to her. She picked it up, turned the volume down. She glanced at the incoming call, hit accept.

"Hi, Beth. What's up?"

"Hey, you, whatcha doing?"

"Writing."

"You're kidding, right? It's eighty degrees. It's Friday. It's time to play."

Kelly Sorenson reached up with her free hand, pinched the bridge of her nose, trying to determine how to keep the conversation from turning the way she knew it was about to go. She loved her friend, but lately, Beth had been on a personal mission to get her a life. And it was driving her crazy.

"Beth…"

"Nope, don't *Beth* me. It's Friday. It's beautiful outside. It's festival time. Come on; we're going out to have some fun. Todd's gone this weekend, and I don't want to eat alone. So you're coming with me. Meet me at Henry's at six!"

Kelly glanced at her watch. Four. That gave her two hours. She could easily make it. She glanced back at her computer, looking at where she'd left off. She'd written at least five thousand words in the last couple of hours, more than enough to keep her on schedule. She could probably squeeze in a few hundred more be-fore she left.

"I hear your brain churning, wondering if you should tell

me no and stay at home and work. The answer is no. Shut your computer down. Get dressed in something cute and meet me at Henry's. Or I'll come get you."

Kelly dropped her head to her hand. Closed her eyes and counted to five. She loved her friend. Beth Watson had been there through the thick of things these past few years. They'd met three years earlier at a writing convention, became inseparable in their few days together. Even after they both returned home, they started a routine of talking once a day, met when they could. They were like soul sisters. They thought alike. They could finish each other's sentences. Hell, they even wrote alike, collaborating on three books to date. But Beth's current mission was truly driving her crazy.

"If I meet you, it'll just be you, right? You don't have an ulterior motive, do you?"

"Geez, I set you up with one bad date, and you're all over me. That was last week. Forget it already. I told you I was sorry."

"Beth, he felt me up. In the restaurant. With you and

Todd on the other side of the table. I'd known him for all of twenty minutes. He was a first-class creep with a capital C. Never again, you got it?"

"Hey, I didn't expect him to do *that*. He's really nice at the club. Todd's played squash with him for months. I have no idea what his problem was."

"Honestly, I'm okay. I don't need a man in my life. I'm really okay."

"Kelly, I know you are. But I just think you work way too much. Trust me; no other writer can dare keep up with your schedule. You're a writing maniac. But you have to live too. You're too young just to sit in your house and write. You need to get out and have fun. You're only fifty-three years old. I know life's been rough since Tom. I get that. Having someone in your life again would be good for you. You're too young not to have the time of your life. Tom would want that for you, you know."

Kelly swallowed, pushing the knot that always formed in her throat back down. Tom. She missed him so much.

Three years earlier, she and Tom had moved to Portland from San Francisco, partly to be nearer to their only daughter who had decided to make Portland home and partly for the opportunity Tom found to head a tech startup. They looked at it as their reinvention, their chance to do something fun and completely out of character.

And so Kelly wrote. She no longer needed a job - the startup bonus and stock option Tom had received ensured that. Her bucket list had always included a line item of becoming a famous novelist. So the move gave her the chance to write.

She nailed it. Killed it. Her first novel was an instant success. She'd hit Amazon and New York Times' best sellers lists within weeks.

They lived a fairytale life. They'd traveled every weekend, visiting Seattle, Vancouver, the coast. They explored the best restaurants. They found a quaint condo in the middle of the city center, remodeled it and called it home.

Then eighteen months later, Tom was on his way to a meeting. A young woman texted her friends, crossed the yellow line, and the fairytale ended, poof, in an instant.

Kelly couldn't have survived it without Beth.

Now she wasn't sure if she'd survive Beth. This dating thing truly was going to kill her. If she didn't kill Beth first.

"No, you can't kill me. It's against the law." Beth snickered, knowing full well what her friend had been thinking. "Come on. Let's meet at Henry's. You love it there. It's always lively, and they have great food. We can check out the latest happenings, watch the younger crowd hit on each other. It'll give us some-thing to write about." If Beth knew anything, it was how to punch her friend's buttons.

"Well, when you put it like that …" Kelly laughed. She loved Beth. And no matter what, she could never stay mad at her for more than a moment. Besides, the weather was truly beautiful. And since Henry's was only ten blocks from her condo, the walk would do her good. "Okay, six, I'll see you there in just a bit."

"Yeah. I'll see you there. Don't be late."

Made in the USA
Monee, IL
06 November 2021